# MOTHERS OF ENCHANTMENT

## NEW TALES OF FAIRY GODMOTHERS

Anthology Edited By

KATE WOLFORD

World Weaver Press

Published by World Weaver Press, LLC
Albuquerque, NM
www.WorldWeaverPress.com

Cover layout and design by Sarena Ulibarri
"Cinderella and her Fairy Godmother" by Edmund Dulac
Other elements used under license from DepositPhotos.com

*

First edition: April 2022
ISBN-13: 978-1-7340545-6-9

Also available as an ebook

MOTHERS OF ENCHANTMENT

# TABLE OF CONTENTS

# INTRODUCTION
Kate Wolford

She's tall and elegant, or tiny with a dowager's hump. Maybe she's dressed for a soirée at Versailles or she's a tired-looking poor old woman who asks nothing more than to have a drink of fresh water from a well. She has many faces, and is often not even a "she," as men are sometimes cast in this role.

This fabled creature is, as you've already guessed, the fairy godmother. We remember her best as the generous fairy who dresses Cinderella and handles transportation while she's at it. But that's just the most famous fairy godmother's tale. Baba Yaga is a fairy godmother with a sense of rough justice, rewarding good heroines with what they need to prevail. The fairies in "Diamonds and Toads" and Mother Holle stories are in the vein of Baba Yaga, as they punish unkind young women as equally as they reward their kindly sisters.

With just a little more imagination, you'll find that fairy godmothers/fathers abound in other tales in a less obvious way. I consider Rumpelstiltskin to be a highly misunderstood fairy godfather. He wants a child, and we don't know that a baby wouldn't be better off with him or the baby's actual parents: A terrified mother who was willing to bargain away a future child to save her own life and a greedy father who was willing to kill a hapless miller's daughter if she couldn't produce the gold he wanted.

Then there's the fairy in "Beauty and the Beast," who ultimately creates a beautiful future for the haughty, vain young prince she makes a beast. You could also argue that the little fellows from "The Elves and the Shoemaker" are fairy godfathers, as they create a prosperous future for the very grateful shoemaker, who, in turn, gifts them with clothes.

The appeal of the fairy godmother/father lies in our wish that someone might appear, and, with a tap of a jewel-encrusted wand, transform our lives with money, status and great clothes. Better yet, the stories appeal to our sense that someone might notice our own good deeds and reward them, as far too many of us do feel that in this tough old world, no good deed goes unpunished.

Yet I think that there is greater appeal in being the magical godparent. What a joy to transform the lives of others with a simple gesture. What a thrill to know you've helped make someone's dreams come true. The good news is, most of us have fairy godparents of a sort, even if they aren't truly magical, for many people transform our lives with simple generosity and kindness.

Perhaps you've been in the position to give a neighbor kid the chance to build a lawn care business. Or, you're the teacher who saw through a sullen student's mask and suggested books that made her really think for the first time. Or you're the aunt or uncle who allowed a nephew to stay with you for his senior year of high school so he wouldn't have to move away from friends. Maybe you've befriended a lonely senior citizen who's now part of your extended family.

In any case, the magic of transformation and support is interwoven throughout our lives, and we usually don't even realize it. Luckily, the authors in this anthology have channeled magic and found gold, and you'll see that these dozen stories will enchant you and inspire your dreams.

In "Wishes to Heaven," Michelle Tang mixes a fairy godmother in truly unusual form with a pregnant woman who loves her husband and her life with him, but is in dire need of help in the most basic ways. The path Tang takes to manage the story is fascinating and, frankly, unique in my reading experience.

In "A Story of Soil and Stardust," Kelly Jarvis takes us to snowy Russia, and interweaves fairy godmothering, family dynamics and justice, with a special doll and an appealing protagonist to make for a delightful read that sweeps you away. And the dynamics between sisters is riveting in Jarvis's story.

"Real Boy" by Marshall J. Moore is another sweeping story that takes a familiar fairy tale and spins it into a saga of creation, flight, loss and confusion with a satisfying ending. The best thing I can say about this engrossing story is that it was inspired by my least favorite fairy tale. That Moore could overcome my antipathy to the inspiration for his work is testimony to the quality of the story.

Lynden Wade takes us into what it's like to be a fairy godmother in "Returning the Favor." You'll fall in love with the fairy godmother in this story, who is wise and loving. And you'll get a peek into what happens to a fairy godmother's charge after the "happily ever after." Most of all, you'll be startled by the form of the fairy godmother. It all works.

Elise Forier Edie brings wit, adventure, humor and exasperation in "My Last Curse." The ambitions of a too-hopeful and overly controlling Queen make this story great fun to read. And our protagonist is a delightfully sassy fairy in a very unusual form. (Fairy godmothers in unusual forms is a terrific theme in this anthology.) It's all good fun. Forier Edie's work has appeared in other anthologies I've edited, and you'll see why when you read "My Last Curse."

"Face in the Mirror" by Sonni de Soto explores "Beauty and the Beast" from a surprising vantage point, with engrossing results. I don't want to ruin the story for you by saying which other fairy tale it reflects, but I can say that making friendship rather than romantic love the basis for this entertaining and heartwarming story was the best choice.

Vivica Reeves weaves loss, love, snow and warmth together artfully in "Forgetful Frost." The pain of loss and the intensity of true love and parental dedication made this an unforgettable story. Reeves' words get you in the gut in the best possible way, and the protagonist is an especially touching character.

Carter Lappin's "Modern Magic" is a candy-colored slice of fun involving lattes, smart phones, garbage and bunny slippers. Sounds fun, right? It is fun. You'll enjoy the modern fairy godmother and her protégée as well as the many charming touches that make this story a light and entertaining read.

"In the Name of Gold" by Claire Noelle Thomas, takes us through the deep pain and sacrifice of one of the most beloved fairy tales. The power of ink and quill and true love and friendship make this story shine like gold, and in the end, you'll feel you know the story Thomas's work is based on in a new and unforgettable way.

Maxine Churchman's "Of Wishes and Fairies" spins elements like a lost princess and a loving foster mother with the trials and errors of a brand-new fairy godmother to create a sweet and satisfying tale with a happy ending—which is just the ending it should have. You'll enjoy the fun and lightheartedness of this story.

Kim Malinowski's "Flick: The Fairy Godmother" blends struggles with anxiety with household chores, serious battles and a titular heroine who is always doing her best despite the challenges she faces. You'll remember Flick, and the brews she ingests to make herself feel better long after you've finished reading her story.

"The Venetian Glass Girl," by Abi Marie Palmer rounds out this delightful dozen with a story of exquisite craftsmanship, envy, skullduggery and bigotry into a highly readable and satisfying story that takes you to Venice and its canals as well as a glassblower's workshop. You'll be swept away.

Before I sign off, there are some people I'd like to thank: Sarena Ulibarri, editor-in-chief of World Weaver Press, who is gracious in the face of the challenges that beset me during every book I edit. Amanda Bergloff, who is essential to my sanity at Enchanted Conversation: A Fairy Tale Magazine, was a great help with editing and formatting the manuscript for this book, and I am most grateful for that.

My husband and daughter, and her family, are always great sources of inspiration and love in every creative endeavor I take on, and this book is no exception. My grandson Ben gives me a great incentive to put together books that he will someday enjoy. I thank them all.

Finally, the readers and writers at Enchanted Conversation make me want to do my best because their love of fairy tales and folklore rivals my own, and they have my gratitude.

May this book bring you as much joy as a tap of the wand from your fairy godmother.

# WISHES TO HEAVEN
## Michelle Tang

Far downhill from Mei-Jin's small house, near the docks, the townspeople celebrated the lantern festival. She stood alone on the hilltop, shivering and wistful. The noise drifted up to her cold ears. Firecrackers snapped and voices sang, and every window in the expensive houses and shops blazed with light.

The crowd released the lanterns together. Hundreds of paper parachutes floated upwards as their reflections sank into the sea. There were so many that their light seemed to lift the shroud of night from the sky; they rose so high Mei-Jin imagined they might become stars. Mei-Jin held onto hers a moment longer, rubbed a finger against the plain rice paper wrapped over the thin bamboo frame. She couldn't spare the expense to buy the one she'd wanted—the one that glowed with colors like flowers beneath the sun.

"I wish my child to have a blessed life," she whispered, a hand on her belly. She threw the lantern up. It teetered for a moment in the air. Her breath caught. Wind righted the paper globe and it ascended, carrying her hopes with it.

"That was an expensive wish." Jun came out to drape a shawl over her shoulders.

"It will be worth it." The small sphere floated upwards, towards the heavens, until the flickering flame disappeared from sight. She prayed her ancestors would hear her amidst the hundreds of other pleas tonight.

Mei-Jin opened her back door and gasped as something swooped near her face. She ducked her head as a moth flew inside. It landed on the worn kitchen table, almost blending in with the faded brown wood.

"Pest." Jun took his slipper off and raised it in the air.

"No. Wait." She took a cup and approached the winged creature. It turned towards her, not moving even an antenna. "It's cute." She placed the cup over its round, fuzzy body and slid it towards the edge of the table onto the flattened palm of her other hand.

"If our ancestors hear you, tonight of all nights, they will make our baby come out with wings." Jun laughed and kissed her goodnight before bending to do the same to her stomach.

Once the moth felt the night air, it fluttered its wings and flew away. Mei-Jin took one last look at the sky before she went to bed.

Two months later, in mid-April, a blight struck her young vegetables. Mei-Jin kneeled on the cool ground, the withered plants limp between her fingers. She wept until the soft soil became wet. The fish Jun brought home, the ones too small to sell for a good price, was barely enough to feed them. They needed the greens she grew—they couldn't afford the produce sold in the market. Something soft touched the back of her neck, feather-light, and she shook her head in irritation.

"I can help you," an old woman's voice said.

Mei-Jin leapt to her feet and looked around, but there was no one in sight.

"Here."

She followed the voice to her shovel. On the handle, a brown moth sat, antennae waving as though in greeting.

*Perhaps I have heat stroke. Or maybe it's the pregnancy.* Mei-Jin went inside to drink water. When she looked out the kitchen window and saw brown earth instead of green leaves, she began to weep again.

"Let me help you, child."

Was it a ghost? Mei-Jin stood and backed out of the room, shrieking when something moved in the corner of her eye. It landed on the table: the moth had followed her inside.

"Is it you talking?" she asked, feeling silly.

The moth bobbed up and down. "Of course. Sit down, please. No need to be so formal with me."

"Why—" Mei-Jin swallowed and tried again. "Why are you here, talking to me?"

"I told you. I want to help. I will grant you three wishes."

"But why do you want to help me?"

The moth's voice sounded surprised. It spoke slowly, as though worried the woman would not understand. "Mei-Jin, you asked for help."

The lantern festival. Hope, long buried, sprouted within Mei-Jin. "I didn't expect a moth."

"What better creature to find floating lights in the night? Think of me as your Fairy Godmoth."

"You mean Fairy Godmother."

The insect fluttered its wings. "Godmoth."

"Were you the one that Jun almost killed?"

"Indeed, and had you not saved me, I would not be here to save you."

Mei-Jin's mind considered dozens of possible wishes. Should she wish for a healthy baby, for her garden to grow, or for enough cloth to sew new clothing? She wanted to choose wisely.

"Will you guide me with my first wish, Fairy Godmoth?"

The moth waved two front legs wide. "I have never been asked that. I would be happy to. What do you think you'd like to ask for first?"

Mei-Jin looked out the window again. "I would like my child to always have enough food and money, starting from now until the end of her days."

"Well-worded, child. Tonight, after you finish your dinner, I want you to bury the fish bones in the garden, and some beneath the fruit trees." The brown insect flew away then, shaking iridescent powder from its wings as it did.

She told Jun about the three wishes when he arrived home, smelling of fish and seawater. He stared at her, brow furrowed, until she finished, and then he said gently, "Perhaps we should have you visit a doctor, for a checkup."

For the rest of the night, Jun continued to glance at Mei-Jin in concern, but she refused to speak again of the moth, or the three wishes. Her mind was made up, and she would not be dissuaded. When she went out to dig up the dirt, he took the shovel from her hands. "You point, I'll dig."

He dug deep holes in the soft soil of the garden and in the hard earth at the base of the fruit trees, grunting as his shovel blade caught blades of grass, blowing on his hands as blisters formed.

She scattered fish bones in each hole and shooed her husband back into the house, using her own hands to push the dirt back where it belonged.

The next morning, Jun, who awoke each dawn to go fishing, shook her out of a deep sleep. "Mei-Jin, Mei-Jin, you have to see this."

The plants were visible even in the dim light of the rising sun. They ran outside, exclaiming at each discovery. The tree branches were bent with fruit, each one large and ripe and flawless. Mei-Jin took a bite of crisp pear and gasped as the cold, sweet juice spilled down her chin. Her garden teemed with vegetables: snow peas and their tender leaves, vibrantly green; potatoes, large and heavy with starch; zucchini, as large as her arm, their skin shining and unblemished.

"I'm going to send Wan Ran and Wan Lu to help you harvest everything," Jun said as he left. "Keep what we need and try to sell the rest."

The neighbors, twin sisters, came by an hour later. They worked until the late afternoon, until their shoulders and backs ached from bending and reaching. Finally, all the ripe fruits and vegetables were in baskets.

"Please, when you go home, tell everyone that we have produce to sell." Mei-Jin gave each girl a full sack to take home.

Soon, a line of people snaked its way up the hill, all clamoring to buy her harvest. Jun returned home, holding three small fish, and ran to wash and change his clothing. Together, they sold all the vegetables and fruits. They held the coins in their hands, more money than they'd ever seen in their lives, and spent the rest of the night dreaming about what they could buy.

"The fish bones must have fertilized the soil. If only we'd known about this earlier, Mei-Jin. We could have been well-fed years ago." Jun tucked the bag of coins safely under a floorboard.

"It wasn't just the fish bones. It was my Fairy Godmoth." He hummed a neutral sound, but Mei-Jin knew he didn't believe her.

The next morning, Jun crowed with such delight Mei-Jin thought it was a rooster. She went to the window to find that all the fruits and vegetables they had picked yesterday had regrown, as ripe and as perfect as before.

He sent the two sisters to the house again. The day was spent like the last, with townspeople coming in droves.

Mei-Jin and Jun soon had to find new hiding places for their money, and they no longer worried about food. "Thank you, Godmoth," Mei-Jin said each morning, before she went out to harvest the garden's riches.

***

Months later, Mei-Jin woke in the middle of the night. The wind carried strange voices from the hill into their open windows. There were men nearby, men with deep, hushed voices and breaths that huffed with exertion. She crept to the front window to peek. The six strangers wielded metal blades that gleamed in the cold light of the moon.

Mei-Jin went to shake her husband, but stopped when she saw his peaceful sleep. She couldn't tell him about the armed men—it would be sending him to his death. Instead, she slid open the window screen and whispered into the night air. "Please, Godmoth. I have a second wish."

The brown moth flew in a moment later, over the heads of the men. They had neared the front door.

"I wish that no harm will come to us in our home." Mei-Jin held her swollen belly with trembling hands.

The insect shook its small wings, and powder fell onto the window sill, glittering like powdered gold. "Take the two pebbles stuck in the bottom of your shoes, and throw them outside. Hurry now, before they come in."

Mei-Jin did as she was told. As she watched, the two tiny pebbles began to shift, growing until they stood as high as the men's shoulders.

"What magic is this?" one of the men said. He backed away.

"They're just stones. What can they do?" The largest man shoved his broad shoulder against the closest one and tipped it over with a ground-shaking impact.

The boulders, for that is what they had become, roiled and strained, rolled and stretched, until they took on the form of lions. The giant cats stalked towards the robbers, reflecting the moonlight with their alabaster skin. The animals pounced and swiped, so fast Mei-Jin's eyes couldn't track them—one movement blurred into the next in streaks of white-grey. The beasts opened their mouths wide and roared challenges at the intruders, but no sound escaped from their airless bodies. The largest man struck out at one with his knife, cobra-fast, but his blade shattered against the solid stone of its chest.

The intruders abandoned their plan and fled, some of them tumbling down the hill in their haste, and the two lions moved towards Mei-Jin's front door, settling their haunches onto the ground and becoming stone once more.

"These guardians will remain here and will come to life at the first sign of danger to your home," the Godmoth said.

Mei-Jin turned on a lamp. She fell on her knees before the moth, bowing deeply with respect. "You saved our lives, Fairy Godmoth. How can I thank you?"

The insect ignored her, bumping against the lampshade again and again.

"Fairy Godmoth?"

The brown moth turned away from the light and returned to the window sill. "My apologies. Sometimes I get distracted."

"How may I repay you for these three wishes?"

The moth moved slower than the last time Mei-Jin had seen it; its wings seemed to lack its old lustre. The old woman's voice remained bright with energy, however. "There is no debt to repay. You made a wish during the Lantern Festival, and I am here to grant it." It turned this way and that, as though taking in their small, sparse bedroom. "You know, you should fix up your house a little bit. Make it nice for the baby, and spare no expense. For you, money grows on trees."

Jun stirred, turning in his sleep to reach for his wife. The moth crawled through the open screen. "You have one wish left, Mei-Jin. Think on it carefully. And you should close this screen. You wouldn't want any insects to fly in."

The moth took wing, soon swallowed by the night's darkness. Mei-Jin rubbed her eyes; she turned off the lamp and slid back into bed. The baby began to hiccup inside her, and she fell asleep to the gentle tapping from within, dreaming of winged old women riding lions that gleamed like knife-blades.

***

Mei-Jin grew bigger as the weeks passed. The August sun made her dizzy with heat, and so she sat and watched the workers tend to her trees and small plot of land in the morning, and then she sat and watched as the produce was sold off in the afternoon. Every day, at least once, she thanked her Fairy Godmoth and wondered what her third wish should be. She had everything she wanted, and more.

"You don't need to go fishing anymore, Jun." Mei-Jin yawned and cracked open an eyelid. "Come back to sleep. The garden will feed us."

"What happens when autumn comes, dear wife?" He finished dressing and leaned to kiss her goodbye. "When the leaves fall and the earth slumbers, the fish sellers must remember me."

The morning passed without event, but in the late afternoon, heavy clouds rolled overhead. It became as dark as dusk, except when lightning flashed across the purple sky. The thunder cracked so near that the ground seemed to tremble, and the sisters Wan Ran and Wan Lu clapped their hands over their ears and sought shelter beneath the trees. She sent the two girls and the other workers home; this was no passing summer storm that would blow over in minutes.

Inside her house, Mei-Jin bit her lip as the wind blew fruit from branches. She stared out the front window, watching for Jun to come dashing up the hill, ducking his head from the rain, but he didn't appear. She worried and paced until her back and swollen feet ached, until she could no longer see through the deluge of rain against the window.

Then, she pushed open her front door, fighting against the howling wind, and waited there. Her eyes strained to see past the furious storm and the gathering dark. She stood for hours, heart in her throat and prayers on her lips. The rain drenched her, the wind chilled her, yet still she stood, as if Jun's safety depended on her keeping vigil.

Night fell. Mei-Jin, chest heavy with fear, decided on her last wish. Suddenly frantic—why had she waited so long?—she screamed into the raging tempest for the moth. The wind snatched away her words. The drumming rain drowned out her voice. Blinding lightning mocked her small lamp. Mei-Jin screamed until she was hoarse, and then screamed some more.

The small brown moth flew in, collapsing in a puddle by her feet. Mei-Jin gasped and scooped it up with her hands, as gently as she would a flower petal, and rushed inside. She blew on the wings and the furry body to dry it, chastising herself all the while. How could she be so selfish? Of course an insect couldn't fly in this weather, and yet here her Godmoth lay, movements weak and few.

"I'm so sorry, Fairy Godmoth," Mei-Jin wept. "I didn't think of your safety. I was so scared for Jun."

Its voice creaked with age, but it held no anger. "That is your third wish, child? The health and safety of your family?"

Mei-Jin swallowed hard, to push her shame and guilt down her throat. She didn't want to ask this of her Godmoth, not when it was so frail, but she pictured Jun lost at sea, and her child growing up without its father, and she steeled herself. "Please, Fairy Godmoth. Save my husband, and keep us all healthy and safe."

The moth twitched a wing. "I…cannot fly in this form. My wings are too damaged." The old woman's voice paused, and when it spoke again, it did so gently. "Mei-Jin."

It was the first time the insect had used her name. "Yes, Fairy Godmoth?" she whispered. It was going to tell her that Jun was gone, that it couldn't help her, that she was a widow. She clenched her eyes shut as if that would protect her from the truth.

"Mei-Jin, you have to kill me."

"Wha—? Fairy Godmoth, how can I do that?"

"I am dying already, child. Look at me. If you want your last wish to come true, you must kill me."

"If I… Jun is alive then? There's still time?" She opened her eyes, but her vision was blurred with tears.

"Not much time left. We have to hurry." The moth crawled closer towards her. "There. Use the cup near your hand, and be quick about it."

It was the same cup she'd used to save it, three wishes and a

14

different life ago. Mei-Jin pressed her lips together and shook her head, clenching her eyes shut once more. "I cannot. Please, you've done so much for us. There must be another way."

"There is no other way, Mei-Jin. But do not worry. This is a mere vessel. You will see me again, and know that I am still helping you."

"But why? How can I see you again if I crush you?" Time was running out, yes, but this was her last chance to get answers. Already her trembling hand gripped the mouth of the cup and raised it in the air.

"The lanterns you release are not only to carry your wishes up to the heavens, child. They guide visiting spirits home. And if a spirit should hear a wish and desire to grant it, they must take a physical form to remain. Now, quickly. You must choose. Questions, or your husband's life."

"Thank you for everything, Godmoth. I'm so sorry." Mei-Jin brought the clay cup down so hard it cracked. She wanted to be sure the insect did not suffer.

She waited, mind racing, heart heavy with fear and hope. Time passed, the minutes distended and pregnant with expectation. The baby kicked once as though to reassure her. Mei-Jin's hands pressed flat against the fine dark wood of their new table; she stared at Jun's empty chair and bit her lip to keep it from trembling. Was the last wish made too late? Had she killed her Fairy Godmoth for nothing?

From the wildness of the storm, a voice howled her name. She ran to the door, shivering as the night's air chilled her sodden clothes. The voice called again, louder than the drumming deluge, carried by the furious wind. Mei-Jin screamed her husband's name, her words stolen from her mouth by the tempest before it reached her ears. Then, like a fish leaping out of the sea, he emerged from the wet night. She embraced him, noticing with alarm how he shook, and rushed him into the house to give him hot tea and warm clothes.

"Mei-Jin, I thought I was going to die. My boat broke apart in the storm—I was hanging onto stray boards for hours." Jun held the teacup in both hands to steady it enough to bring to his blue-tinged lips. "The sky was so dark and the waves so high. I couldn't see the way to land."

Mei-Jin shuddered at the thought of him swimming further away from shore, until his arms failed and his legs became anchors. "How did you come home? What happened?"

Jun shook his head, eyes so wide she could see white all around his brown irises. "A glowing light appeared in front of me. It spoke to me, and I followed it to safety."

"That was my Fairy Godmoth." Mei-Jin glanced away from the cracked cup, still on the table where she'd left it. "I told you it was real."

She understood the expression on Jun's face now: she'd never seen it before, but he was awestruck. His voice was reverent. "Your Godmoth—the light that saved me—had my grandmother's voice!"

\*\*\*

Mei-Jin screamed again. This time, another voice joined her, the weak cry clinging to the strong. The midwife checked the newborn as Jun hovered, his crushed fingers still gripped in Mei-Jin's sweaty grasp.

"She's so tiny." He cast a worried glance at the woman cleaning his child. "She came out too early."

"Aye, and her lungs are frail. But the baby comes when it comes." The midwife thumped the tiny back, much harder than Mei-Jin thought necessary. The mewl that rose from the baby's pink mouth had a wet, strained sound.

"She is born too close to all soul's day. This is a bad omen," Jun moaned, his voice low and mournful.

The baby was placed on Mei-Jin's chest, and she met her daughter's dark eyes. Mei-Jin traced loving fingers over the baby's dark hair, the perfect shell of her ear, and down the soft fuzz of her back. She paused, wiped tears away and looked again.

Her laugh startled the midwife and Jun out of their furrowed brows and furtive whispers. "She's going to be just fine, our baby. Look."

In the middle of the newborn's back, between her two little shoulder blades, was a birthmark. It resembled a brown moth spreading its wings.

They named her Fei, which meant "to dance in the air." On her one hundredth day of life, Jun invited the townspeople to their renovated house.

"The house is so much bigger. I can't wait to see what you've done on the inside," one of the fishmongers said.

"The two stone lions don't look so out of place now," teased another.

"Her one hundredth day celebration falling on the same night as the lantern festival—what luck!" The lantern seller handed Mei-Jin her finest work as she entered.

"They don't need any more luck. It's February and still their garden grows fresh vegetables every day." The merchant clapped a large hand on Jun's shoulder and laughed.

After they handed out red-dyed eggs, devoured the banquet, and everyone had greeted the baby, the townspeople made their way back outside. The stars blinked overhead like a waiting audience. Mei-Jin held out Fei's lantern, colors as vivid as flowers in the sun, and bowed until her forehead pressed against the bamboo frame.

"Thank you for making all my wishes come true, Fairy Godmoth." She let her baby touch the rice paper, once, and then set the glowing globe aloft. It rose into the dark sky alone, a second moon, before the others released their lanterns. The rising ceiling of flames made the night bright as dawn, and Mei-Jin lifted her face to marvel at the sight. Jun leaned over to kiss his wife and daughter.

A brown moth flew by, landing on Fei's thick blanket. Mei-Jin held her breath, but the insect didn't speak. After a moment, it flew upwards, high enough to bat against Fei's lantern.

"There are so many moths, Mei-Jin. Imagine how many spirits are being guided to heaven tonight."

There were dozens of the winged creatures, in different shapes and sizes, attracted to the floating balls of light. Some, like the brown moth, seemed to stay around a specific paper lantern; others danced from one to another before flying back down to earth.

"I hope all your wishes are fulfilled." Jun said to each of their guests as they left.

"If you find a moth in your home, be gentle with it," Mei-Jin called out, snuggling Fei close. Her daughter slept, safe and healthy and loved. The baby's soft hair tickled Mei-Jin's cheek, like a moth's wings fluttering against her skin.

*** 

**Michelle Tang** writes speculative fiction from Canada, where she lives with her family. Her short stories have been published in several anthologies, including *Terrifying Ghosts, Night Terrors, Vol. 2,* and *Once Upon an Enchanted Forest.* When she's not writing, Michelle enjoys watching horror movies, napping, and lurking on social media.

# A STORY OF SOIL AND STARDUST
Kelly Jarvis

A waning crescent moon rises in the midnight sky, its pale rays casting silver shadows across my bloodied hands.

If my *krestnaya*, my godmother, could see me now, surrounded by the splintered remains of my hazel tree, she would throw her head back and laugh like a madwoman.

The melodic chime of the Great Clock signals the end of the Autumn Festival. The old gossips will already be gathering in the kingdom kitchens to season their stories over steaming cups of spiced tea.

They will speak of a girl so good and kind she wore dresses spun of the sky. They will speak of a girl so good and kind she captured the heart of a Prince.

They will sprinkle goodness and kindness like seeds across their firm dough of lies, and the famished villagers, enticed by the smell of stories baking like bread, will scramble to savor the first sweet bites of their *sushki*.

It is true I wore a dress that shimmered with the shades of sunset. It is true I danced with a Prince, and my beauty took his breath away.

But only my godmother knows the whole truth.

I have never wanted to be good, and I have not always chosen to

19

be kind.

***

Kindness was easy, in the beginning.

I remember the enchanted winters of my childhood when wind and ice waltzed outside our windows. I watched the snow swirl from my little chair beside the hearth, warmed by the love of my mother and grandmother who tended the cozy fire which crackled in the grate.

My most treasured toy, a *matryoshka* doll, was my constant companion. I liked to trace my finger over the swirls of painted poppies circling the wooden doll's waist, and then twist her open to find her replica inside. Another twist would reveal a third, even smaller copy, a tiny round egg that fit into the hollow of my hand.

My father, a soldier, had longed for a son. He was stationed far from home, and I rarely saw him. He would spend his holiday leave with us, his shining medals filling our cabin with blinding light. He would kiss my grandmother's cheek and sweep my mother off her feet so that she lost her breath from laughing, but I was shy of him, and his presence made me so sullen that the skies filled with threatening clouds.

"Do not cry, Eleonora," my grandmother would say when my father would turn me away from my mother's bed where I was accustomed to sleep each night. My grandmother would let me rest with her until dawn when we would rise to cook the pancakes for our morning meal. We would roll the tender circles in butter and jam and, when day broke and my father had eaten, he would return to his regiment and the sky would clear once more.

In the springtime my grandmother's garden bloomed like magic. Pink peonies and yellow golden root shone like jewels against the green of the forest, and rows of onions grew beneath the ground, their papery skins hiding layers of sweet juicy flesh. In the summer, my mother and grandmother would take me to splash in the shallows of a shady pond where tiny minnows sparkled in the setting sun.

One evening, we lingered so long that the moon, waxing gibbous, met its reflection in the water. The three of us joined our hands, an unbroken circle in the summer twilight. Fireflies blinked above our heads, bathing us in an iridescent glow. "The magic is inside you, Eleonora," my grandmother whispered, and I shivered as the cool night air kissed my dampened skin.

\*\*\*

It was the magic inside my mother which was growing that evening, and by the time the leaves turned rusty, she was round with child. Her pregnancy tired her, and she spent long hours in bed. To keep me still, my grandmother taught me to sew by casting patterns of silvery stars across thick scraps of fabric. "Follow the stars," she told me, and I pulled my ebony thread from star to star, stitching galaxies and constellations through the squares of cloth.

Late one night my mother woke me from sleep. The full moon, surrounded by a faint ring of dusty light, hung in the sky just outside our bedroom window. My mother's face was flushed, and her breathing labored.

"Elya," she moaned, using my pet name from infancy. "If you are a good girl and say your prayers, I shall look down on you from heaven and always be with you."

Her words frightened me. I did not want to be a good girl. I did not want to say my prayers. I wanted my mother.

My grandmother lifted me from the bed and ushered me out of the room.

"Be a good girl, Elya," my mother wailed. "Be kind," she cried, as if her entrance into the afterlife depended on me.

The wind howled, and I felt an icy chill as death crossed the threshold of our dwelling.

I closed my eyes and began to pray.

I did not want to be good. I did not want to be kind.

But I promised the gods that I would try.

\*\*\*

My sister was born in the early hours of the morning. Death attended the birth, and carried her spirit away. I never saw her, though I was told she looked like me, small and dark, my tiny replica, who would have fit inside me like a *matryoshka* doll.

My mother died that morning as well, though she never stopped breathing. She buried herself in grief, and her soft, warm glow, which was the center of my world, faded into a cold, distant silence.

My grandmother laid the baby to rest in her garden. It was long past planting time, but when she whispered words of enchantment over seeds of chamomile and chrysanthemum, the blooms blushed, pink and white, in a circle over the grave.

"We must place your sister in the earth, for that is how she will rise to heaven," my grandmother explained. The next day, I found a dead bird along the edge of the forest path. I dug a hole and sang enchantments over it so that the buried bird might soar to eternity. Two weeks later, I returned and unearthed the bird's little grave.

Its broken body was still there.

*** 

My father arrived for the New Year, bearing gifts he said he had gathered from Grandfather Frost. There was a tin of dried apricots dipped in chocolate for my grandmother, and an enameled cross to hang about my mother's neck. In my box, beneath layers of purple tissue paper as thin as onion skins, was a cloth doll with a china face framed by silky golden curls.

My parents spent the day together while I wandered through the forest alone, dropping stones into the frosty pond and watching the cold water ripple outward in endless circles. I returned home when evening fell, hungry and hopeful that my grandmother had prepared my favorite meal, *sochivo*, a thick porridge topped with walnuts and fruit. My parents, impatient with my tardiness, were waiting in their traveling cloaks. My expensive new doll lay upon a small black bag which had been placed by the door.

My father had taken a new position in the capital city. His success would provide our family with luxuries. The three of us were to leave immediately, before the winter storms shut down carriage travel in the rural part of the kingdom.

I did not care about luxuries. I wanted to stay in my home with my grandmother. I wanted to be close to my sister's grave where the pink and white flowers would always bloom.

I began to scream and cry; angry drops of ice thundered down on the roof. I picked up my cloth doll and shattered its face on the stone hearth. Shards of fine china flew across the room.

"Enough, Eleonora," my father shouted, and his powerful voice scared me into silence. He roughly raised me into the back of the waiting carriage which was already hitched to his horses. He helped my mother into the front and flicked his riding crop so fiercely that the horses broke into a spirited trot. I watched as my grandmother, standing in the doorway of our little cabin, faded away in a whirl of frozen rain and tears.

***

Our new home lay in the shadow of the Great Castle. From our front window we could see the spires crowned with opulent teardrops in every color and pattern imaginable. The Great Clock in the city square pealed out the hours, and everywhere was the sound of soldiers marching and the cry of shopkeepers selling their wares.

My room was so large that even my soft voice echoed, and the silk sheets on the bed were so cold that I struggled to sleep. I would carry my blanket to my bedroom hearth, seeking what little company the civilized flames had to offer.

My father held audience with the Tsar himself, and the noble classes were curious to learn how our family had risen to social importance. Finely dressed gossips would stop by for tea, thirsty for information they could serve to families throughout the kingdom.

The gossips told my mother the Tsar had a young son who would need to be married one day. They persuaded her to haul me out for inspection like a prime cut of meat.

I had been dragging my fingers though the ashes on my bedroom hearth, tracing galaxies and constellations in the cinders. Soot streaked down my face and dress, and when my mother saw me, she turned white with embarrassment.

"Soiled-Elya," she scolded, signaling the nursemaid to return me to my room.

The gossips laughed politely, already peppering their tales. "Some children grow into their beauty, and even a girl who is not beautiful can make a kind and pious wife for the prince."

\*\*\*

Life in the busy city suited my mother. She and my father made a stunning couple, and their presence was requested at festivities throughout the visiting season. I would watch from the shadows as they left for parties, my father, tall and striking in his uniform, and my mother, beautiful in her brocade ball gowns, the hems floating over the marble tiles.

Before long, my mother was once again with child. I was in her bedchamber when the baby, another girl, arrived like a glorious sunrise. She was pink and fat and lovely with a row of silky blonde curls framing her face. I stroked her tiny hand, and her fingers curled around mine. I fell in love with her before I even learned her name.

When my father, who had spent the long birthing hours at a local tavern, burst unsteadily into the room, I leaned across my mother and sister to protect them from his disappointment with another daughter.

The baby turned to look at him and blinked her brilliant blue eyes.

"*Nasha printsessa*, our princess," he muttered, his breath stale with alcohol. He gently caressed her, as if she might shatter.

Then he noticed me.

"You are full of ashes and soot." He swatted me away from the baby. "You will clean yourself before you come near your sister again," he commanded, pulling me off the bed.

"*Mamoosya*," I cried out because I was scared and did not want to leave my mother's side.

But my mother could not take her eyes from their princess. She cradled my sister and spoke lovingly to her.

My father closed the bedroom door behind him, leaving me alone in the vacant hall.

\*\*\*

My sister grew more radiant with each passing year. Our mother delighted in displaying her for the old gossips who continued to visit, and my sister would twirl for them, her yellow curls bouncing.

"She will make a beautiful wife for the prince," the old gossips said, simmering their new stories to perfection.

On nights when our parents were called away, my sister would snuggle next to me in bed while I told her of our grandmother's magic garden in the forest. Once we stayed awake far past our bedtime, giggling so loudly that our mother, still wearing the furs she had donned for that night's engagement, came to investigate.

"What are you doing awake?" she asked coldly.

"Are you talking about me?"

When I didn't answer, she gathered my sister into her arms. "*Nasha printsessa*," she cooed, "you must not sleep with this soiled girl. Come, you may spend the night with your Mama."

\*\*\*

When my sister came of age, our parents planned a lavish party to introduce her into society. Moments before she was to make her entrance, my sister ran into my room on the verge of tears.

"Elya," she pleaded. "I can do nothing with my hair!"

In spite of her tears, she was exquisite. I sighed deeply, but began combing out her hair, winding glittering crystals into her wispy yellow curls.

My sister watched me in the mirror. My own raven colored hair, which had been cleaned and brushed for the occasion, pooled around my shoulders. It was my best feature, inherited from my mother, and my sister had always been jealous of it.

"No one is here to see you," she hissed, suddenly hostile. "You are Soiled-Elya. You are Ashy-Elya."

I pulled her curls so hard her head jerked back.

She spun around to face me. "Cinder-Elya!" she screeched.

I slapped her. The angry red outline of my hand swelled upon her cheek.

My sister's brilliant blue eyes widened in silent surprise, and then she began to scream.

The guests were already arriving. It was too late to cancel the party. Excuses for our absence would have to be made.

My sister, her bruised face swollen with tears, would not be twirling for anyone.

***

I was not called down to face my parents until well past midnight when all of the guests had left. I passed by the dining room where the smell of smoked pork lingered; discarded silver platters were piled high with shortbread and layered honey cakes.

My father, in his full military regalia, loomed over me.

A small black bag had been placed by the door.

"You are being sent to apprentice with your godmother, Eleonora. The sun will not rise on another day with such a disobedient daughter in my house," my father sneered.

"I have no *krestnaya*, no godmother," I said, beginning to shake with fear.

The wind howled around the spires of the Great Castle.

"Please," my voice was unsteady. "I have no godmother!"

My mother, who had been standing in the shadows, took my hands in hers. "Of course you have a *krestnaya*, Elya. She is your grandmother's sister, and she was my midwife when you were born." She spoke softly, and my childhood name on her lips brought me to tears.

"I will be good. I will be kind," I promised. "*Mamoosya*, please do not send me away!"

My father said nothing but forcefully escorted me across the foyer. One of his soldiers helped me onto the back of a horse, and we galloped through the stormy night at full speed until the familiar sounds of the city gave way to the distant howl of wolves.

***

"My godmother?" I asked timidly when the soldier pushed me down to the ground on an abandoned forest trail.

"Baba Yaga lives in the clearing," he answered gruffly, redirecting his horse and returning the way we had come. "I have taken you far enough."

Baba Yaga.

I remembered the stories my nursemaids would tell me when I first arrived in the city, a petulant, unruly child, who refused to do as they asked.

"Perhaps you would rather be sent to live with Baba Yaga than stay in a fine house like this one," they would chastise me. "Baba Yaga is the long-nosed witch of the woods who flies through the night in her mortar and pestle, sweeping away proof of her evil deeds with a broom made of silver birch."

Their stories always ended with the same terrifying threat. "If you do not behave, Baba Yaga will cook you in her big black pot and eat you up for dinner."

Baba Yaga was nothing more than a story to frighten naughty little girls.

I heard the distant thundering of hooves on the muddy trail, and hoped my father's soldier had taken pity on me and returned. Instead, I looked back to see a monstrous man atop a pale horse laden with heavy packages. The rider wore a colorless coat splattered with dirt kicked up by the frantic trot of the horse, and his long white hair streamed behind him as he urged his ghostly stallion forward with his whip. I cowered in the shadows of the trees until he passed, shivering in the gust of frozen air that lingered on the trail.

When I found the courage to follow the fading stars toward the first streak of dawn in the eastern sky, I reached a small clearing. I felt as though I had wandered into a picture painted by the ghoulish words of my nursemaids. I saw a fence built of bones, its rusted gate swinging on a shrieking hinge. Lanterns made of human skulls sat atop the posts and their light cast hideous shadows across the ground. Behind the fence, a hut constructed of rotting wood rose from the earth. A flock of dirty fowl clucked noisily against its walls, and it seemed as though the house swayed and danced on chicken feet.

The sound of a horse approaching overtook me once more, and I feared it was the return of the ghostly rider who had come to claim my soul. I looked back to see a man even more menacing atop a chestnut steed. I sobbed as his horse slowed and stopped before me, its hot breath curling around me like smoke.

Time stood still as the rider rubbed a calloused hand over the auburn stubble of his face and followed the curves of my body with his bloodshot eyes. When the sun broke the horizon, bathing us in a red, angry light, he silently dropped a heavy satchel onto the ground and turned to ride away.

A soiled old woman with a long nose and wiry gray hair stepped onto the porch.

She held a broom made of silver birch in her hand.

\*\*\*

"I am called Elya," I whispered when I could bear the witch's silent gaze no longer.

She sniffed the air and her wrinkled pink tongue darted over her lips, wetting them with a film of glistening saliva that made my blood run cold. Her beady black eyes assessed me, and I felt as though she could see directly into my soul.

"Eleonora," she said my full name slowly, savoring it before she swallowed. "I know your mother and grandmother well."

She scraped her dirty fingernails across the handle of her broom. "Carry in the satchel my red rider has left by the gate and come make yourself useful."

She turned her bony legs toward the house and then looked back at me over her shoulder.

"If you can't be useful, I will eat you up for dinner," she added, as though she were the connoisseur of my nursery cuisine. She threw her head back and laughed at her own cleverness, her horrifying cackle recoiling off the crooked limbs of the trees.

The satchel was wet and leaked a warm brown liquid onto my hands. I set it down on the floor beside a white leather package overflowing with half burned and broken branches.

"I'm hungry, bring me whatever's in the kitchen," my godmother demanded, lowering into a little wooden chair and stretching across the length of the table. The chair groaned as it supported her weight, and for a terrifying moment, I imagined the chair was a living being forced into servitude by my *krestnaya* as penance for some long forgotten crime.

A cast iron stove smoked in the corner. The spicy scent of sausage rose from a skillet, and a thick porridge bubbled in a big black pot. Loaves of fresh rye bread cooled on the sideboard next to pots of butter and sour cream. There was enough food for ten people, and my stomach lurched. I had not eaten since before my sister's party, since before I had struck her face and been sent away.

I set a steaming plate of food before my godmother, and she shoveled spoonfuls into her mouth, smacking her lips. When she had eaten her fill, she eyed me suspiciously, and then passed me a moldy crust of bread and a discarded scrap of ham too tough for her to chew.

"Thank you, *Krestnaya* Mama," I murmured as I choked it down.

Baba Yaga yawned. I could see the remains of her breakfast clinging to her sharp teeth. "While I rest you will clean the hut, sweep the yard, wash the linen, cook the supper, and sort the branches."

She pinched my arm and leaned so close to me that I could smell her sausage breath. "If you can't be useful, I will eat you up for dinner," she repeated, so pleased with her humor that she laughed until she fell asleep and filled the little hut with the rattling sounds of her snores.

***

When Baba Yaga woke, I served her dinner, though I ached with my long day's toil. I had prepared enough food to feed my father's famished soldiers, and though I was dizzy with hunger, I had not tasted a bite for fear of what my godmother might do to me.

She gulped a mug of *kvass*, letting the brown droplets run down her chin as she moved on to the roast chicken, her tongue expertly stripping the meat from the bones. Her eyes roamed over my domestic handiwork as she ate, and they came to rest on the untouched package of burned and broken branches.

My heart rose up into my throat.

I wanted to tell her that I did not know how to sort the branches. I wanted to tell her I hated her horrible hut in the woods.

Baba Yaga narrowed her eyes and read my ungrateful thoughts as if I had spoken them aloud.

Suddenly, the branches flew out of their package, knocking against my head with such force that I fell to the floor. A massive book dropped heavily into my lap. The cover was made of tree bark, still sticky with sap, and the thick, waxy pages moved up and down as though they were breathing.

"Everything you need is inside you, Eleonora."

My godmother picked her teeth with a chicken bone.

"You can eat when you are done with your tasks," she added cruelly, feeding my meagre portion of discarded dumplings to the black cat curled at her feet.

My hands were shaking. The wind outside began to whirl. The heavy book spoke aloud as I opened it, relaying its secrets about the trees of the forest. The hazel tree, grown in the darkest part of the woods, would bring about great change. The white birch, its bark spotted and rough, should be used for renewal and cleansing.

Darkness fell long before my task was complete, and a third rider in a black hooded cloak arrived. He led his inky horse directly to the front door and delivered a writhing parcel tightly wrapped with twine. I thought I heard the cry of a frightened child, but the sound was muffled by my godmother laughing defiantly, her head turned up to the expansive night sky.

***

It was days before I finished sorting the branches. A group of peasant women, their faces hidden by shadows, arrived to sand them smooth and whittle them into wands. Their hands dipped the branches in oils and carved ancient symbols into the bark bases. Baba Yaga made me separate the finished wands into dusty jars which lined her pantry shelves.

My godmother used the wands when frightened villagers came to her hut, begging for help. "Better you should learn to help yourselves," she would hiss at them, and then she would set them to impossible tasks to win her favor. Sometimes she required them to secure the dried blood of a gray wolf or the clippings of a newborn baby's hair submerged nine days in vinegar. Other times, she forced them to bring her sacred items that had been gifted to them by their adversaries. Only if they took part in her rituals would she agree to assist them, choosing the wands best suited to the dark needs of each magic spell.

One day, my godmother dumped a metal bucket full of damp earth on the newly swept floor of the hut and commanded me to separate the poppy seeds from the soil. My hands and face were streaked with days of dust and tears before I discovered water would make the seeds float away from the dirt.

I boldly slammed two buckets on the table in front of her, one filled with the separated soil and the other with the deep black poppy seeds floating in water I had hauled from a nearby stream. I was tired of her senseless tasks.

She flashed an evil smile and casually dumped both buckets back to the floor. The water, soil, and seeds swirled together again, leaving a thick smear of filth on everything they touched.

"A seed cannot grow without soil, Eleonora," she said, laughing wildly as she shoved a broom into my shaking hands.

\*\*\*

As the dark time of the year approached, Baba Yaga spent more time away at her wicked gatherings. I began to read her books and snoop through her private spaces. Beneath her mattress, I found a *matryoshka* doll, painted with bright poppies, exactly like the one I had at my grandmother's house when I was a child.

I twisted the doll open two times and held the smallest piece in my hand. I returned the doll's outer shells to their hiding spot, but I kept the tiniest doll in my pocket, an unkind act of defiance that brought me strange comfort.

I sometimes noticed Baba Yaga looking at the pocket of my dress, and I shuddered to think what my *krestnaya* would do if she knew that her goddaughter was a thief.

When the winter holidays neared, I asked my godmother for leave to visit my family. She was enjoying her favorite, beef stroganoff in rich gravy, and she belched in response, wiping her mouth on the sleeve of her shirt.

"Not every question has a good answer. If you know too much, you will soon grow old."

She slapped a letter down on the table. It was addressed to me and written in my father's heavy script.

He hoped I was well and that my ordeal had taught me to be a light to our family. There was no need for me to visit for the winter holidays this year. My mother had taken ill, and there would be no parties, no presents, and no celebrations.

In my memory, I could hear my mother begging me to be good and kind as she had on that night so long ago when she fell ill and lost her baby. My father's instructions to stay away from home were drowned out by the echo of those urgent cries.

"My mother is ill. I must go to her." I met Baba Yaga's stare with determined eyes.

"So, my thieving goddaughter wants to go home and be her mother's blessing."

A massive winter storm suddenly descended from the tranquil sky. Hailstones rained down on the roof and the forest trees creaked and groaned. The little hut began to spin in circles, sending dishes and cups rattling across the room and knocking me off balance.

"I want no blessed daughters here!" Baba Yaga shrieked. A great gust of wind blew open the front door and snow streamed into the kitchen, the flakes biting into my skin like sharp iron teeth.

"*Krestnaya* Mama, godmother, please!" I cried, but she mercilessly pushed me out into the storm. The bone fence already buckled under the weight of fast falling snow. I fell through the gate and into the frightening jaws of the forest, my godmother's sadistic laugh chasing me as I ran.

***

I expected to find my parents' house shrouded in the silence of sickness, but when I approached the door, light and music poured from the windows. Dozens of guests toasted the New Year with gleaming cups of champagne. My mother, aglow with health and happiness, smiled at my father and sister.

I stood, shivering and alone behind the frosty panes of glass, as the three of them joined their hands, an unbroken circle in the flickering candlelight.

***

I did not enter my parents' house until all the guests had departed. I wanted only to go to my room and sleep for a hundred years, but my sister dragged me to a table topped with sweet breads and tea, eager to show me the holiday gifts she had received from our parents.

"Of course, I still need pearl combs for my hair," she pouted, not bothering to ask me about my long journey or offer me a sweater to place over my damp, dirty rags.

My father smiled indulgently. He would be taking a trip which would keep him away from home for several months. If his princess was very good and kind while he was away, he would bring the pearl combs just in time for the visiting season when the prince was rumored to be choosing his wife.

"You must bring Eleonora a present as well," my mother said, her voice thick with guilt, as if a gift would make up for the fact that my parents no longer wanted me.

I knew my father's journey would take him through a grove of low-hanging hazel trees. It was the only way in and out of the city during the winter snows.

"Bring me back the first branch that brushes against your hat," I said.

My father's lip curled in disgust. "A stick will make a fitting gift for our soiled daughter."

"Soiled-Elya, Ashy-Elya, Cinder-Elya," my sister sang, the familiar tune wrenching my grief-stricken heart.

This time, I did not react in anger. I kept my hands to myself.

I let them think I had learned my place. I let them think I wanted nothing but a stick.

Soon enough, they would learn the truth.

What I wanted was a wand.

*** 

My father did not return from his journey until the spring thaws, the time of planting magic. I snuck away to a small patch of untouched greenery on the outskirts of the castle grounds. The hazel branch my father had begrudgingly gifted me trembled in my hands.

I scraped the bark off the stick, revealing the smooth wood beneath. I carved swirling symbols into the base and rubbed its length with oils I had taken from my mother's dressing table. Then I took the tiny *matryoshka* doll I had stolen from my godmother and buried it with the hazel shavings deep in the soft, black, soil.

Each day I spoke enchantments, circling my wand around the sacred space. Soon, a hazel sprout, fresh and green, found its way from beneath the earth. I watered it with my tears until it stretched to the skies above me and sheltered me like a mother protecting her only child.

\*\*\*

When the Tsar announced the annual Autumn Festival, I did not beg for permission to attend as I had in years past. I did not wish for a fairy to help me dress for the ball. It was better for me to help myself. My godmother had taught me that.

I went to my hazel tree, and, with my wand, I pulled down the brilliant blue color of the sky, stitching the air into a gossamer gown that poured over me like liquid. A little white bird flew down from its nest in my tree and spread its downy plumage across my eyes, transforming into an ornate mask which would hide my identity. Two white birds fluttered their wings across my shoulders, creating a feathered cloak to protect me from the cool autumn breeze.

When I entered the castle on the first night of the festival, all eyes were upon me, though no one knew my name. The Prince danced with me until dawn, but that is a tale I need not tell, for it will be told a thousand times.

I cast a veil of smoke to help me escape, leaving everyone in the castle ravenous for more.

\*\*\*

On the second night of the festival, I arrived in a velvet dress woven out of the sunset. It shimmered as I moved, its soft magenta hues swirling with shades of azure and indigo above slippers crafted of glass.

The crowds salivated as the prince twirled me across the dance floor, but I made my exit before they finished feasting upon my romantic story. I could hear their hungry souls still rumbling as I took my leave.

I came face to face with my sister on the castle steps. Her eyes widened in confusion when she recognized me. My masking spell had been strong, but my sister had always shown signs of having our family's gift of sight.

"Did Mother make you that dress?" she asked.

Her elaborate gown and precious pearls looked faded and dull next to the living light of my clothes.

She grabbed my hair in anger, and I tumbled down the stone steps.

The air turned crimson as a flock of red feathered birds with beady black eyes flapped forward to rescue me from her attack. Their talons tore my sister's dress to shreds.

When they finally flew away, she lifted her hands to her face.

Thick clots of blood dripped down from her once brilliant blue eyes.

\*\*\*

I did not return home until the next evening. My sister lay asleep on the couch, a bloody bandage over her face.

"So, my soiled daughter has decided to come back." My mother frowned at my dress which had disintegrated into common rags.

"Will she be alright?" I asked, my voice thick with guilt.

"The Prince has decided to marry," my mother said, ignoring my question. "He has recovered the glass slipper of the most beautiful girl in the kingdom. He has vowed to marry the girl whose foot fits into the slipper. He will be here tonight, after the close of the Autumn Festival, to find his true bride."

"The slipper will not fit her," I said.

"She will not need to walk when she is queen."

My mother held a kitchen knife in her hands, and I did not need our family's sight to see my sister's future.

I backed away toward the door, my eyes still searching my mother's expression.

I wanted to ask her if I might be the mysterious girl who had proven herself worthy of the prince's love, but I suspected

her answer would carve sadness into my soul and make me grow old
with knowledge.

***

The melodic chime of the Great Clock falls silent.

The Autumn Festival is done. A black bird separates itself from
the night, waning crescent moons winking from the deep wells of its
eyes.

My hands, soiled and bloodied from uprooting my avenging hazel
tree, cradle the unearthed *matryoshka* doll I stole from Baba Yaga. I
trace my finger over the swirls of painted flowers circling the doll's
waist and uncover a hidden indentation. She is too small to hold a
replica inside, but I twist her until she opens.

In the curve of her wooden womb is a single poppy seed.

It is a kernel of potential. It is a harbinger of new life. It is my
story, waiting to be written.

I think about returning home to slide my foot into a glass slipper,
to let the Tsar's son spirit me away to my happily ever after. I think
of my sister, blinded by jealousy and bleeding for her chance to
become Queen. I think of the beautiful way my mother and
grandmother once loved me, and the bloom of pink and white
flowers over an infant's grave. I think of my godmother, the long
nosed witch of the woods, who manifests her own magic and laughs
at the twisted tales others tell about her.

I hold my breath a moment, letting my godmother's wisdom wash
over me. Then I make my choice to laugh with her, my head thrown
back in defiance toward the enormity of the sky.

In the wind, I can almost hear the old gossips as they roll out their
dough of story, hastily adding new herbs to balance the salty taste of
this unexpected ingredient. Their recipe has been handed down for
centuries, but each generation must substitute spices as circumstance
demands.

When I was small, I fed upon their tales, wishing a fairy
godmother would shape me into the sugary mouthful that my mother

wanted me to be. How lucky my godmother turned out to be a witch who taught me it is better to eat heartily at the table of life than allow myself to be consumed by another's hunger.

I point my wand at the bird perched on my broken hazel tree, stealing its inky color to sew myself traveling clothes and boots as black as evening. I turn the bird's claw into a pewter pendant that clutches a crystal globe of light, and loop it through a necklace I fashion from the silver strands of the moon. I place the poppy seed into the hollow of the crystal and hang the chain around my neck. Then I drop the empty shell of the stolen *matryoshka* doll in a deep puddle and watch as the cold water ripples outward in endless circles.

I take a deep breath of the autumn evening, sniffing the air like my *krestnaya*, my godmother, who can smell the future on the breeze. The scent of the forest, which holds the decomposing past within it even as it brings forth new life, will point me in the right direction.

I know my family will not look for me.

I know I will never stop wishing that they find me.

I lift my wand to the stars, pulling their twinkling beauty down from the heavens in a spiral of incandescence. A storm of stardust swirls around me and becomes a billowing cloak that sparkles like the Milky Way.

I turn away from the kingdom of my childhood and move toward the first blush of dawn in the eastern sky. Drops of stardust unfurl from my cloak like a trail of breadcrumbs in my wake, stitching a map of constellations and galaxies into the ebony soil beneath my feet.

Those who wish to taste the truth of my tale will find me by following the stars.

\*\*\*

**Kelly Jarvis** works as the Special Projects Writer for *Enchanted Conversation: A Fairy Tale Magazine*. Her poetry has also appeared in *Eternal Haunted Summer* and *Mermaids Monthly*. She teaches literature, writing, and fairy tales at Central Connecticut State University and Tunxis Community College.

# REAL BOY

Marshall J. Moore

Perhaps it was unwise to give life to a lifeless thing.

My intentions were good, if not wholly honest. I can at least admit that much. Certainly, I could not have reckoned the amount of harm you would inflict, both to others and to yourself. I would have prevented it if I could.

That is the heart of the problem, I suppose. My people are a people of great power but little wisdom. We can transmute lead into gold as easily as a man turns water to waste, and with as little thought. At a whisper from us, frogs and birds may speak the tongue of man, but we pay little heed to what secret mysteries of nature that such unwary speakers might reveal.

It is a consequence of immortality, I think.

We are creatures without end, you see. No blade can pierce us, nor can a bullet bite us. We eat and drink when it amuses us to do so, but have never known the pains of thirst and hunger. Disease cannot touch us, nor age diminish us.

This, I think, is where our reputation for cruel tricks and deadly pranks originates. We pass the eons in little feuds and petty vendettas, amusing ourselves with such idle sport. And if a mortal stumbles its hapless way into our domains, how could we help but treat him similarly?

Understand, cruelty is not our intent. We simply underestimate the frailty of mortal bodies, the speed with which they succumb to blows or age. A hundred years of dancing in a masquerade is a fine thing to us, but a mortal invited to such a ball will return home to the death of all they have known and loved.

How can a being that can never know pain, that will never die, judge the consequences of her actions? Being myself a stranger to harm and suffering, how could I predict when they might befall one of mortal kind?

You think I am making excuses. Perhaps I am.

Let me try to explain.

Mine are a sensual people; our greatest joys are those of touch, of flesh against flesh or cool air over bare skin, of sunlight on our faces. Our bodies may be as unending as the Earth, but we have never ceased to take pleasure in them.

Only one pleasure is denied us.

There have never been any faerie children. Nor shall there ever be. That too is a consequence of our nature. Any race that dies not, yet still sires offspring, would inevitably breed like rabbits until we covered the earth like weeds. There are no fathers among us, no mothers. No daughters and no sons.

Perhaps that is why I made you.

Strange that I had not thought of it until now.

Which brings us, of course, to the man who named himself your father.

***

He was elderly, as you know: a bent old man with a round belly and thick spectacles. But the eyes behind those lenses were blue and clear as a robin's egg, and his hands were sure and steady despite his years.

In his youth he had been handsome, though all that remained of his looks were bright apple-cheeks and a kind smile. Despite his looks, he had never taken a wife—in fact, he had no interest in women at all. Ordinarily such men in this time and place become men of the cloth, but his small village already had a priest, and no need of another. Though he remained a bachelor, he nonetheless pursued the family trade and became a woodcarver.

A poor man, but a skilled one. His hands had known chisel and pick since the time he had learned to walk. Where other children were given toys, he was given a saw and awl. The carving knife was to his hand what the paintbrush was to Michelangelo.

You know all this, of course. You were born in his workshop, surrounded by the works of his hands.

Fine furniture he made: chairs and stools both sturdy and comfortable, and tables that would not sag under the burden of a lordly feast. A new pulpit for the parish priest of rich mahogany, and a crucifix for the village widow to hang from her door.

All he made with careful attention, for like all great craftsmen he put the love of his art into his work. Yet he remained poor, for his heart was kindly, and he gave freely to those with little or less than himself, never reckoning what he was owed for his labors.

But most marvelous of all were the toys: little soldiers standing in their battalions, marionettes that moved with the fluid grace of living things, and a rocking horse fit to be a prince's steed. These he gave away freely when he might have sold each for a duke's ransom, and by the children of the village he was much beloved.

He was a kind soul, your father. Even I could see that, and my understanding of human beings and their natures is admittedly limited.

Which is why I chose to grant his fondest wish.

*** 

As I have said, the woodcarver never married. Indeed, the very thought of a woman's caress repulsed him, though curiously he showed as little interest in the company of men as he did women. Perhaps that was the reason for his genius. Lacking the passion of the flesh, he poured himself into his work as ardently as ever two lovers poured themselves into one another.

Make no mistake, his craft was his purpose, and it filled him with pride. He awoke each morning eager to begin his work, tending each piece with the care and patience he would one day devote to you. He took great satisfaction in the way his arms ached at the close of each day, considering the thousand splinters that plagued his callused hands a fair price for making works of beauty. He delighted in the giving of his wares to grateful patrons, in the joy that shone bright as a star upon their faces.

The woodcarver was a simple man, glad to have a roof over his head and a trade that put bread upon his table. In all ways save one he was content.

He was lonely, you see.

That is what drew me to him, I think. In him I sensed something of a kindred spirit. My kind seldom seek companionship, but countless years upon the earth had left me weary of solitude.

Thus I watched him, shadowing his steps unseen for many years. His folk can see mine seldom now, if at all, so I became a silent, constant presence in his home.

I helped him as much as I could, tidying his workshop when he fell into bed too tired to put away his tools, and bringing him a pillow and blanket when sleep claimed him at his desk. Bronze and silver coins of little worth I hid amongst his tools and in the pockets of his jacket, knowing that he would think these small windfalls were merely his earnings from his work, absentmindedly misplaced. And in a thousand other little ways I eased his days.

Yet a ghost makes for poor company, and so his loneliness persisted, until one clear winter night.

He knelt beside an open window, clad only in a nightshirt yet heedless of the cold wind. Tears streamed down his face as he clasped his wrinkled hands together and prayed to God and all the saints for a son, so that he might have someone to care for, to teach his craft and the love of it so that the works of his hands would not fade from the world once his time came to an end. His tears splashed against the floor as the cold clear stars shone brightly outside the window, deaf to his pleas.

I do not know whether any god or saint heard the old woodcarver's prayer that night.

But I did.

*** 

The woodcarver had labored over you for the better part of a year. He had carved you carefully from a fine young cypress on the border of his village. Like all artists, he saw the finished work within the raw material. He took you home and set you in a place of pride in his workshop, foremost among all the half-finished furniture and rough sketches.

Other orders there were to fill, so your development was slow and halting, yet each day he set aside an hour to tend to you. I watched as he pruned you like a young tree, smoothing a rough patch of bark here, shaving off a wayward splinter there.

At first you were no more than a block of wood, a thick stump of tree-trunk that looked more suited for kindling than for what you would become. Yet day by day he whittled away the dross, and slowly you began to emerge.

Like most newborns, you came into the world headfirst, the crude sphere that would one day become your face emerging from the uniform block of wood. In those early days you resembled nothing so much as a chess-piece; a pawn.

Perhaps it was an omen of what you would become.

The roundness of your head was marred only by an obstinately outthrust knob; the beginnings of a branch, had your tree remained unfelled. The woodcarver carefully shaped your emerging face around it, and so even from the first your nose was given particular prominence. Your cheeks he painted apple-red, perhaps wishing to impart some resemblance to himself to his wooden child. Why else would he paint your eyes the same bright blue as his own?

Slowly, a day at a time, the rest of you began to emerge from your block of wood. Your father carved each piece of you separately, devoting as much care to the shape of your limbs and the sturdy barrel of your torso as he did to the features of your face. Each joint of your fingers was made with all of his delicate attention to detail and the gentle ministrations of his own rough hands. God Himself could not have formed Adam with greater care.

Only after months of labor were you fully finished, on the very morning before the woodcarver knelt before his open window and prayed to whoever might be listening. And oh, you were beautiful. Your arms and legs were of burnished cypress, handsome and smooth. Your face was earnest and cherubic, the round cheeks and guileless eyes the very picture of innocence. Looking at you one almost thought you might rise and speak of your own accord.

What a surprise for the woodcarver, then, when you actually did.

\*\*\*

From the first you were a wicked thing.

Perhaps that is my fault. I was not what one might call a doting parent. I suppose most first-time mothers are, but you must remember that I am not human.

Then again, neither are you.

Like God upon the seventh day, I rested once my labor was complete. My power is not without its limits, and your creation cost me a great deal. So I took the smallest form I could, one that would allow me both to rest enough to recover and a way to keep an eye on you. I became a little blue cricket, lurking unobtrusively in the walls of the workshop.

The woodcarver, overjoyed to find his dearest wish fulfilled, clothed you and doted on you as though you were the child of his body rather than the work of his hands. He began to teach you his craft, but you were disinterested, often interrupting him with inane questions. "Why is the sky blue? Why do things fall down? Why is your hair gray?"

To his credit, the woodcarver answered each question with the patience native to his trade, though always he would redirect your attention to the matter at hand. Yet it soon became apparent that distractibility was only the least of your flaws.

Not knowing how the world might react to a talking, walking marionette, the woodcarver kept you hidden away inside until he could figure out a way to explain you to his neighbors. You quickly grew bored of the woodcarver's little world, of his humble workshop and the tiny loft above it where he slept. And like any child cooped up and bored, your idle hands soon turned to mischief.

You began to steal things from your father, taking his tools when his back was turned and hiding them amongst the clutter of the workshop. At first it was merely a nuisance to the old woodcarver, who blamed the sudden disappearance of his chisels and picks upon his own absent mind. But soon it became a matter of concern, as clients who had never before had cause for complaint grew irritated with the delays caused by your little pranks.

Kind soul that he was, it was long before he began to suspect that you might be responsible. And when he asked you if you had seen his awl, you shook your head and told him no, even though the awl was at that very moment in the pocket of your overalls.

Few things trouble me, but that did. The woodcarver was an honest man, and I had spoken to you only once, when I brought you to life and bade you be good to he who was to be your father. Where then had you learned to lie so baldly? Not from either of us.

Even then, I hoped that the lying was an aberration, not a symptom of a deceitful nature. You were new to the world, and were only just discovering the power of words, and how they need not always be true. Still, something would need to be done to rectify your lies before they became habitual.

Recovering as I was from my labors, I lacked the strength to set a geas upon you. But I could at least hinder you, and so in the voice of a chirping cricket I wove a spell upon you as you slept.

The next day you hid your father's mallet, stowing it away in the cupboard where he kept what little china he owned. Without it, he could not finish the table he had spent the past week making for the parish priest. He spent better than an hour searching for it, turning his workshop upside-down in the process. At last, weary and defeated, he turned to you and asked you if you knew where his mallet was.

"No, Father," you said, and to the surprise of you both your nose grew a full inch.

He looked at you, puzzled, as you gingerly touched your newly lengthened proboscis.

"My son," he asked again, "did you take my mallet?"

This time you merely shook your head, wary of another outright lie. But my spell was cleverer than that, and your nose grew another inch.

"Are you lying?" he asked, his mouth a thin frown beneath his mustache.

"No!" you squeaked. Your nose was now as long as one of the old man's fingers.

"My son," he repeated, the kindness in his voice never wavering, "was that a lie?"

The silence of every child caught with his hand in a cookie jar followed.

"Yes," you said, and your nose shrunk by an inch.

Swiftly you confessed to every item you had ever hidden away, until your nose had returned to its previous size. The woodcarver was greatly saddened by your deceit, and with a heavy heart he bent you across his knee and spanked you for every tool you had taken. I watched silently from the rafters of the workshop, satisfied that I had prevented you from further mischief.

How wrong I was.

*** 

I suppose all children run away from home at some point, though most never make it farther than the borders of their neighborhood.

Still, each child holds in his heart the desire for a horizon other than the one he has known his whole life long, the wandering freedom of unknown vistas and undiscovered wonders. And the woodcarver's workshop was a very small neighborhood for a child as inquisitive as you, puppet or not.

So perhaps what followed was inevitable.

One damp spring night the woodcarver fell asleep at his desk, leaving the door unlatched. You draped a blanket over him and slipped out into the wind and rain, shutting the door tight behind you.

You did love him, after all.

It may be that I am too harsh on you. I do not know your heart, so perhaps I am too quick to judge. I can hardly fault you for wanting even a glimpse of the world beyond the workshop walls. You may not have even meant to truly run away. Perhaps you only wished to explore for a few hours while your father slept, returning before the break of dawn with him none the wiser.

I do not know. I did not ask, after all.

But I did follow you. You were my creation, and my responsibility, though in my present state I could do little either to protect you or guide you. Still I trailed you, flitting my way between raindrops in cricket guise as you ambled up the dark and empty streets, taking in the high gables and painted walls of the town with wonder in your eyes.

No lights shone in the windows above you, for it was late into the night. A warm yellow glow spilled from only one low building at the bottom of the high street, drawing you hither like a moth to flame. From within came sounds of carousing and merriment. Eager to make your first acquaintance of those who were not your father, you unlatched the door and stepped inside. A small blue cricket hurried after, leaping inside just as the door shut behind you.

The inn was warm and raucous, full of men's rough laughter and jeering voices. No one noticed a small cloaked figure make his way across the room, towards the center of the commotion.

A makeshift stage had been erected in the center of the inn, and upon it danced a troupe of marionettes: Clever Harlequin, absurd Pulcinella, greedy Pantalone. They moved jerkily and gracelessly, their capers and japes tired and uninspired, but the crowd of drunken men laughed and cheered them nonetheless.

You, of course, were fascinated. Your father had explained to you as best he could how you were not like other boys, that you were a marionette given life rather than a child born of woman. But he had neglected to mention the distinction between yourself and other puppets. After months of cohabitation with the kindly man who was made of flesh, the appearance of these other wooden beings walking and talking just as you did must have seemed like the discovery of a long-lost family.

So enamored were you of your newfound compatriots that you lost your wits entirely, forgetting the woodcarver's warnings about strangers. You jumped onstage as Pantalone was busily stealing the keys from Pulcinella's belt, seizing them from the pilfering puppet and holding them aloft with a triumphant "Here they are!"

The crowd erupted in amazed laughter, thinking it a fine bit of puppetry for one of the troupers to appear from among them. Those not so deep in their cups as the rest marveled at how cleverly your strings were hidden, for stare as they might they could not discern them.

But I had eyes for none of this. Hidden atop the inn's rafters, my eyes were fixed on the Puppeteer himself.

I have spoken before of my folk, of how we are not as men are. Of how we pass the centuries in idle amusements, meddling in the lives of mortals to stave off the boredom of years unending.

The being that lurked above the curtain of the puppet-stage was the worst of my kindred. The misfortune of human beings was ambrosia to him, his own cruelty nectar. His mischief had toppled kingdoms and corrupted saints. Many names he has had through the years, but for your tale the Puppeteer will do.

He was clever as all my race are, recovering swiftly from your interruption. He continued his performance, incorporating your participation as seamlessly as though it had been planned all along. The Puppeteer plied his trade with fae-nimble fingers, until Harlequin and his companions seemed nearly as lively as you were. Still too naïve to understand the trap you had fallen into, you followed eagerly along with the japes of Pulcinella and Pantalone, to the crowd's roaring delight.

At the performance's close you took your bow with the other puppets, but before you could give the game away the Puppeteer dropped the curtain and whisked you to his little room in the back of the inn. I pursued as I could, leaping madly across the floorboards and narrowly avoiding being crushed by stomping feet. I cannot die, of course, but to be discorporated would be a terrible inconvenience.

I slipped under the door of the Puppeteer's room and was immediately encased by a heavy glass jar slamming down on me. I lay stunned as the jar was upended and a lid screwed onto it, the Puppeteer's huge green eye staring evilly at me through the glass.

My haste had made me foolish. He had known my presence, just as I had known his. He had surmised that the animated puppet that joined his troupe was the work of his kin, and now schemed to steal you away for his own profit.

And now I was trapped in a jar, too weak to do anything but beat my wings against the glass as the Puppeteer plied you with brown ale and tales of fantastical places beyond your wildest imaginings. You had never tasted anything stronger than water, and soon you were reeling drunk. Drunk enough to sign the contract he set before you, promising a century of servanthood to the Puppeteer, with the solemn assurance that you were to be treated no worse than any other member of his troupe.

The ink had hardly dried when he let out a huge, guffawing laugh and picked you up bodily, carrying you easily under one arm. You were too stupefied to struggle, and I could only watch helplessly through a window as he tied you with puppet strings and loaded you into the back of his cart, tossing you into a heap beside the now-lifeless forms of Pulcinella and Harlequin. He climbed into the driver's seat and whipped at his donkey until it snorted and started, chortling to himself all the while.

I watched as the cart disappeared into the rainy night, knowing I might never see you again.

*** 

I lost you for a time after that. It took some days before one of the inn's regulars knocked my jar from the table, shattering it and freeing me. I went straight to the woodcarver's home, hoping to find a way to relay to him what had transpired. But the door was locked and the lights were off. He had realized your disappearance and had departed in search of you.

Even now I cannot say where his journey led him—down what strange and lonely roads he wandered in search of the puppet he loved like a living son. I know only that the days were not kind to him, and that by the time we three were together for the final time, he was thin and haggard, half-mad from the trials and hardships he had endured.

It was a long time before I ever saw your father again.

But I am getting ahead of myself.

*** 

You know better than I what transpired in the days that followed. That the Puppeteer soon discarded his wily charm in favor of a more brutish approach, threatening to make firewood of you unless you did exactly as he instructed. That you were kept in a birdcage when not forced to perform, that your pleas to be returned to your home and your father fell upon deaf ears.

What I learned, I learned from tracing your footsteps. The Puppeteer was crafty, but his own laziness and greed played against him. Disregarding any pursuit, his course kept to the larger towns, where his puppet show would earn him bigger crowds and a fatter purse.

You were his star attraction, of course. Everywhere I went I heard tales of the incredible puppet that walked and talked and danced on its own, free of strings. Each town brought me closer to you, but never quite close enough. The puppet show had always just left, not a fortnight before—or a week before, or a handful of days.

Closer, steadily closer, until at last I found you.

***

The Puppeteer was not a perpetually roaming creature. Like certain of my folk, he had made a stronghold for himself; a little demesne so suffused with his power and will that it was no longer wholly of the mortal Earth.

The Island was a den of sin and vice, as you well know by now. Here the Puppeteer gathered all the lost souls he had seduced into wayward mischief, setting them loose upon a place where there were neither parents nor constables to restrain their every wicked impulse.

For you were not the only one he had waylaid and misled, not by any measure. Young boys were his preferred prey, being headstrong and disobedient by nature. It amused the Puppeteer to offer them all the freedom and delight they could wish, allowing them to indulge in every sin and vice that had ever been denied them. The very air of the place was a haze of thick cigar smoke, suffused with the stench of stale beer. The boys ran half-savage about the place, waging little wars when they were not too busy cheating and misleading one another.

In this den of sin and vice I found you, drunk and stumbling, cards in your hand and a cigarillo in your mouth. Other boys jeered and shouted as you diced with them, matching them wager for wager, unaware of what was about to befall them.

I could feel the magic moving in the air; the Puppeteer's will weaving his terrible influence through the boys there gathered. They had fallen deep into their own wickedness, soon to consume them entirely. Even as I landed upon your shoulder, the first of your companions began to change.

His head was thrown back, laughing at some crude jape, when his laughter turned into a braying hee-haw. His mouth lengthened into a crude snout, and his laughter turned into a startled wheeze. He raised his hands to his face, only to find that they had been transfigured into hooves.

Screams and shouts broke out all across the room, though they were swiftly overtaken by donkeys' panicked bleats. All around you fur burst from skin, ears and faces lengthened, eyes grew beady and dull as your companions in wickedness lurched to the floor, stumbling on unfamiliar equine legs.

Even you, wooden though you may be, were not immune. Your painted eyes widened in horror as a tail burst from between your britches, and your ears grew long and furred. I had to act.

In my travels I had regained my strength, though I still held myself in cricket-form, lest circumstances required some sudden expenditure of the power I had slowly regained.

Now, it seemed, was such a time.

I could not combat the Puppeteer's will directly, here in the heart of his strength, but I did what I could to nullify it. I slowed your transformation, holding it at bay even as the room grew full of wild-eyed asses.

"Run!" I hissed in your ear. "Flee this place!"

Startled, you nevertheless obeyed. Together we fled the Puppeteer's Island, untying a wooden skiff from the docks and slipping away into the night, over dark waters with the sound of braying donkey-voices echoing behind us.

*** 

Maybe it was serendipity, then, that we found your father.

I do not know why I am telling you this. You were there, after all.

We fled southwards along the coast, not daring to travel too directly back to shore lest the Puppeteer realize you had escaped his clutches and search the surrounding environs for you. And unbeknownst to you or me, your father was making his slow way north in a vessel of his own, a boat he had spent every penny of his savings to rent from an old fisherman. He had tracked you, slower and more uncertainly than I had, until he had caught wind of the island where lost boys landed.

We nearly missed each other; the proverbial ships passing in the night. Only a restlessness on his part led to his rising and seeing the dark shape of our skiff on the far horizon. He hailed us, his old voice calling clear across the waves.

You slept on, but I heard him calling. In gull's shape I winged across the water to his boat and told him that you slept safely scant yards away. With a cry of jubilation the woodcarver tacked his sail and flew over the waves towards you.

The wind suddenly picked up, growing from a tranquil night to a storming gale in a space of minutes. The woodcarver steered valiantly towards your skiff, where you had woken to the violent rocking of the waves. Scrambling onto the deck, you looked across the water and saw your father for the first time in months.

You called out his name, and he called yours. Tears shone in his bright blue eyes, and you would have cried too if you could.

Despite the battering wind and waves, the woodcarver's course held true. His boat pulled up alongside your skiff, and he reached for you, one hand still clutching the helm. The skiff rocked beneath you, and you nearly slipped from the deck.

Your father's rough hand seized yours, heedless of the splinters you left on his calloused palms. He hauled you onto the deck and embraced you, holding you tight against his chest as the rain washed away his tears. For a fleeting moment, you held one another tight.

Then a great breaking wave rolled across the deck of your father's vessel, swamping the boat. Above us a shadow rose from the depths, towering against the storm-wracked sky above the little boat. It had the form of a huge whale, black as sin, breaching the dark waves. But I recognized the Puppeteer's green eye, and the malice within.

We had not escaped cleanly, as I had thought. The Puppeteer had been aware of my presence as soon as I had arrived on his Island. He had allowed our escape, so that he might destroy both my works and my physical body in one fell stroke.

I suppose that makes what followed after my fault. If I could feel sorrow, I would apologize for it. But what is done is done.

The whale came crashing down, slow and inexorable as a felled tree. The woodcarver stared up in terror, too wearied from his desperate flight across the waves to move.

But you were not. You seized him about the middle and shoved with all the strength in your wooden limbs, throwing you both over the rail as the great whale's bulk smashed both boats into splinters. I followed you over the side, shifting into a seal's shape even as I hit the waves. I dove, tail working powerfully as I slipped under your sinking bodies and pulled you to the shore. The Puppeteer did not pursue, perhaps thinking his task accomplished.

Only once we reached the shore did I resume my human form, dragging you bodily onto the rocky beach. You were shattered and broken, looking less like a marionette and more like so much kindling. Your father looked much the same, save one crucial difference.

His eyes, so clear and blue, now stared blankly up at the sky, unseeing. He was gone.

*** 

And now, here at the end, I stand above your broken and splintered body, musing on whether I erred in your creation.

You lay beside the body of your father, the woodcarver who brought you forth from a block of wood and shaped you with loving care into a form that was very nearly human. A cruel irony that at the end he looks more like a marionette than you do, his limbs splayed and bent at unnatural angles. One hand lies outstretched towards you, his pale fingers almost touching yours. His final act was to try to reach you one last time.

Sadness is not a feeling I am accustomed to. Imagine, living as long as we do, how it would be if we mourned for every fallen oak and withered vine? The grief of uncounted centuries would drive us irretrievably mad. Instead we accept the passing of all things in the course of time, save ourselves. The bodies strewn before me should bother me no more than the passing of the seasons.

And yet.

I feel...*something* for what has come to pass. Responsible, I suppose. Had I not followed the woodcarver through his waking days, had I not granted his tearful prayer. Had I given you my love from the first, tried to lower myself to understand the thoughts and fears and feelings of a soul in a wooden body. Had I done these things, or not done them, perhaps neither of you would be lying broken upon this rocky shore.

You stir feebly, your splintered limbs twitching and jerking as the surf laps at you, beginning the process that will leave you little more than a smooth and featureless hunk of driftwood, given time. Your mouth has been smashed against the rocks, and you cannot talk, but there is no mistaking the fear in your painted eyes as you stare up at me.

I was the first sight those painted eyes beheld. Fitting, then, that I should be the last as well.

I raise my wand, gathering the magic to me as I prepare to speak the words that would unmake you. The broken fragments of your mouth work silently, and your one remaining hand crawls across the sand like a crab. For a moment I think it is a last desperate attempt to escape, to drag your broken self away from your demise. But not for the first time you surprise me.

Your hand comes to a stop beside your father's.

Your wooden fingers curl gently around his.

You look up at me, suddenly still. Only the light in your painted eyes marks you as a living thing.

My hand trembles around my wand, and for the first time since I cannot remember, I hesitate before acting.

Though it was I who gave you life, it was the woodcarver who had raised you. He had cared for you, both before and after you began to walk and talk. He had clothed you, played with you, done his best to teach you wrong from right. He had not done his task perfectly, but he had done his best. Your wickedness at any rate was in spite of his love, not because of it.

And were you truly such a terrible creature yourself? The harm you have done was for the most part unintended. I must remind myself that you are a new creation. Though you have the speech and awareness of a boy of ten, your span of time awake upon the earth is that of a toddler's. Can the ignorant be held to account for the sins they have committed in their ignorance?

You were capable of kindness when the mood struck you. That is a trait we share, though it shames me to think that all you have inherited from me is my own capricious moral understanding. But you had a teacher in your father, the woodcarver, one wiser and kinder to instruct you—as I never could—in the ways of right and wrong.

At the end you risked the peril of your own body to save him. It is not a thing I pretend to understand, but I know the story of the God who became man well enough to know the value humans place on self-sacrifice.

That you failed is no mark against you. If your father the woodcarver had not died today, he might have tomorrow, or in a hundred years. The length of a life has no bearing on its finality. Death comes to all mortals, sooner or later.

But you are not mortal. Not yet.

Or are you?

I remember how even as you left your father's house for the last time, you tucked a blanket over him. You are a mixed creature, a blend of impulses both good and evil, forever striving to fulfill the former while denying the latter. You are neither angel nor devil, but you are striving to become more angelic all the same.

What mortal man, even the best among them, can claim to be any different?

I raise my wand and speak a word of power. For a moment, all the world goes still. The crashing waves behind me subside, the pounding sea growing placid as a mountain pond. The wind ceases to howl, and overhead the cries of gulls are silenced.

I press my wand against your brow, your handsome sycamore skin now chipped and splintered. I leave it there.

The transformation happens slowly, so gradually that the exact moment of change cannot be marked. Its first evidence is the disappearance of your injuries as your shattered limbs reaffix themselves to your battered torso. I watch as your injuries knit themselves back together, your wounds and splinters smoothing themselves over until you are as pristine as when I first granted you consciousness.

And then the true transformation begins.

Your cold body grows warm to the touch as hard cypress becomes soft skin. Your rough edges grow gentle, and your broken jaw is now healed. The straw that served as your hair is replaced by the genuine article, curling gently over your unlined brow. From between your living lips comes a plume of breath in the winter air.

Finally before me lies not the mangled and broken remains of a marionette, but a boy of flesh and blood, as human as the man lying beside him had been.

Last of all your eyes open. They are beautiful, a clear robin's egg blue.

You look up at me and smile. It is not a baby's smile, wide and guileless. Nor is it the smile of one who has seen such things as you have; the haunted smile of the troubled. It is the smile of one eager to run and dance and play, to experience all the joys and pains the day has to offer.

The smile of a real boy.

\*\*\*

**Marshall J. Moore** is a writer, filmmaker, and martial artist. His work has appeared in publications including *Mysterion*, Flame Tree Publishing, Tyche Books, and many others. He lives in Atlanta, Georgia, with his wife Megan and their two cats.

# RETURNING THE FAVOR
### Lynden Wade

*In one of the tales from the thick forests of Germany, a princess saves a prince from, of all things, an enchanted stove, then loses him again when she spends too long saying goodbye to her family. The quest to win back her beloved from his new fiancée is a familiar pattern in fairy-tales. But where other young women are helped by the sun, moon, and winds, or an old crone, in this story she is helped by three toads in a cottage. The conclusion has it that with the breaking of the enchantment the toads are revealed to be the children of kings.*

*The story is wrong on two points. One is the number of toads—there was only one. The other is how the tale ends. I should know: I was there.*

\*\*\*

I am just drifting off to sleep when I hear a knock on the door. I sigh and crawl back out from under my stone. As I hop up the garden path, I suddenly realize what's wrong. My visitors always arrive at night. It was a condition I set up, so I could sleep by day. What's different about this one, then?

My visitor stands on my doorstep, expecting me to be inside the cottage. I can only see the visitor's back. Breeches? What's a man doing at my door?

"One moment," I call.

The figure turns, and I see it is in fact a young woman, a hood slipping off her head, hair bound away from her face. At first I do not recognise her. I think she must be a new quester, another maiden on a journey to find her heart's desire. There is something familiar about her huge eyes, though.

"Grandmother! You don't recognize me. The princess who rescued her prince from an iron stove?"

The title she uses, I must tell you now, is out of respect for my age. I ask all the girls who come here to address me this way.

"Of course! Alina, isn't it?" It's not just the breeches. She looks taller, stronger, her mouth set more decisively. A determined woman, altogether unlike the weeping girl who knocked on my door—I try to count the days in my head—yes, about a year ago.

"That's right."

"But—why are you here? Did you free the prince?" The girls never come back. I try not to let my worry sound in my voice, but I can feel my eyes bulge. Well, my eyes always bulge these days. After fifty years in this shape, I ought to be used to it.

The princess is surely bone-weary from her journey, but I can see from her face that it is not exhaustion that keeps her silent. She chews her lip.

"We'd best go in and sit down. After you."

Alina lifts the latch for us, and we pass into the front room. I keep it warm and cozy, just right for a tired traveler. I'm wide awake now, and equal parts curious and concerned.

"Father didn't want me to come. The journey to find my husband had been so dangerous, he wanted me to stay in safety once I'd returned. But I knew I had to do this."

"And your prince? Surely he wanted you to stay by his side?" I am thoroughly alarmed now. All my girls are meant to live happily ever after. This princess does not look happy.

In fact, now I study her carefully, she looks guilty. "I had to steal out of the window before he'd woken up."

I wait for Alina to explain this, my throat pulsing. When I first took on this role, I would make the mistake of hurrying the girls, of putting words in their mouths. Gradually I realized that it's better for them to form their own tales. That way, they learn what they really want.

"Oh!" A hand flies to her mouth. "You must think I'm running away from him. That I'm unhappy, and ungrateful for all you've done. That's not the case at all."

"Perhaps you should sit down and have a cup of tea with me, just as you did before. Then tell me all about it."

The princess sinks into the chair by the window and I put the kettle over the fire. A toad, making tea, you laugh? I'm no ordinary toad, you must see that by now. I'm more partial, myself, to teas like nettle and linden, but I make sure I keep Darjeeling and Oolong for guests.

You might think I cast a good deal of spells. In fact, I use very few. One that I need each time, however, is tea-making. As I boil the kettle, measure out the dark, dry leaves and fill the little china teapot, each guest sits and waits, and the torrent of words with which she first assails me drains away. As I slide cups into saucers and offer milk and sugar, my guest will pick over the flotsam from her verbal storm for the real desire of her heart.

The girl asks for a splash of milk and helps herself to three sugar lumps. I'd worry about her teeth if I wasn't so worried about her heart. But when she's sipped half the tea in her cup, she puts it down gently in the saucer, and says, "I should be happy. Our palace is so comfortable! The kitchens are always warm and busy, making all sorts of delicious things to eat. You'd have thought my husband would never want to see a stove again, but the opposite is true. He is always planning new recipes, finding new foods to try out. Chocolate buns with cocoa from the rainforests, biscuits full of nuts from the sunny hill country, and pies with apples from the North."

"They sound wonderful. I can only offer fruitcake, I'm afraid.

Would you like a slice?"

"Thank you, it looks delicious. It's not just the food, of course. My husband is kind and generous and loving and we do laugh together! He…" She looked a little abashed. "He likes to hide in cupboards and jump out at me. And then we hide together and jump out at the chancellor."

I laugh at this picture because I think she wants me to, but my anxiety grows. The reason for her discontent will come. I must be patient.

"It's not just silly games of course. There are—he is wonderful to be with in every way." A blush rises from the drawstrings of her hood, up across her cheeks. I nod to show I understand, to save her saying more. In fact, I can't fully sympathize. In the first month of my marriage there were some good times, but it was not the same after my mother-in-law's interference. Still, his love had never been my heart's true desire.

"And he and my father are such good friends. They go hunting together, and beat each other at chess frequently."

She's skirting around the issue. I refill her cup and stifle a sigh. Looking up, I guess from her face that she detected my thoughts.

The words come out in a rush. "For a long time, I wouldn't look at my feelings. I knew I should be happy, with a wonderful husband and a beautiful palace. But something tugged at my heart, and made a cloud between us, like smoke in the kitchen. My prince began to notice that I didn't laugh so much. Then I knew I had to do something."

"So, you're here?"

"Yes. Because—because I can't enjoy my happiness when you, Grandmother Toad, are unhappy."

"Me, unhappy? Why would you think that, my dear? Here in a pretty little cottage with the best tea from the East and the finest bone-china tea set?"

The princess puts her hands on her knees and leans forward. She stares into my eyes. It is not a comfortable experience. "You haven't always been a toad."

I jerk with surprise. My tea splashes all over the linen tablecloth. That will stain badly if I don't wash it soon. "Now you are talking complete nonsense, child."

She shakes her head and her dark hair, escaping from its leather thong, haloes round her temples. "I saw you. When you handed me the gifts for my quest, the needles, the plow, and the nuts, you shimmered, and I saw your true form."

My voice comes out louder than I mean, in order to project assurance, to make her think she's wrong. "You are very fanciful, my dear. What stories you'll have to tell your children."

"I know I am right. Why do you persist in denying it? I want to help you." Those soft brown eyes are very misleading. She knows her mind and will not be swayed.

"That's not the way it works, child. I am old and wise and ugly. I help the young and lost and beautiful to find their heart's desire."

She slips off her chair and kneels in front of me. Her face screws up with thought and she studies me with far more intensity than I like.

"You are not old and ugly. You are a beautiful woman."

A gasp escapes me. I turn it into a laugh. "What a fanciful idea! I think you got a touch of sun-stroke on the journey here."

Her mouth firms. "I barely saw the sun. Most of the way it was windy. I know what I saw—you are enchanted, like my prince. What should I do? Are you able to tell me how to break the spell, just as my beloved told me how to free him from the iron stove? Or must I seek out some other wise being to show me how? I will do it, even if it means climbing more glass mountains, and crossing sea after sea. Even if I have to work as a kitchen maid again."

I study her face, her hands, her feet. I imagine how she finally appeared when she found her prince—sun-burned by half her travels, toes frostbitten by the last miles, hands red and swollen from washing dishes as she waited for a glimpse of him. Such strength she'd discovered, such love she'd shown. I think of the trials I went through once myself, for my own heart's desire. Such different trials, but propelled by the same determination and longing. "Child. What a great heart you have. I only help the pure in heart, but you have shown today that you are the best of all the girls I've helped on their way. Nevertheless, this isn't an enchantment, and so it can't be broken."

She is quiet, then draws in a big breath. "Do you mean... you've *chosen* to be like this?"

What an extraordinary girl. Not just to see my other form, but to discern that I did it to myself. "Yes."

"You chose to be a toad?"

"I did. My role allows me to determine my form—woman, bird or animal. If I was to live in the forest once more, I wanted a body well-suited to it this time." As soon as the words are out of my wide mouth I regret my choices. Why did I say "once more"? Will the phrase betray the full truth? She's only guessed the half.

Her lips open to ask me more, so I interrupt. "I am content, child, truly I am. Now go home to your prince. Have many beautiful, good-hearted children together. Be happy and grow old with him. I hope he values your big heart for its true worth. It does you great credit that you thought of me and came back."

At last she stands up. One hand brushes her hair back, but without really trying to catch it again in its bands. "You're hiding something. But it's your right to keep it to yourself if you choose. I'll do as you say. I'll go home, and I'll enjoy the good things I have because of you."

"Because of your own courage, too, child. My gifts would have been no use to someone lazy or selfish."

"Goodbye, Grandmother Toad."

"Goodbye, Princess. Safe journey home."

I open the door for her. As I always do, I look up at the sky, checking for the flight of swans, forgetting for a sliver of a moment that my brothers are long since dead. The sadness is sharp but brief. The sun has begun to lower through the trees, but there is still enough light to flash off the hard green of holly leaves. A distance away, a white horse, its bridle looped round the branch of a birch, grazes quietly.

The princess walks over to her mount, her feet crunching in the fall of brown leaves. She puts a foot in the stirrup and throws a leg over the horse. With a flick, she's released the reins. The horse prances and swings round, and off they canter. The beat of hooves fades along with the sight of the girl in breeches, and I am left alone with myself.

When I am really perplexed, I find a pond or a puddle. In the calm surface, I can see a reflection of my former self. We talk, my woman self and my toad self, and we resolve my worries. Today I hop to the small pool near the edge of the woods, and lock eyes with the female in the water. After a few steadying breaths, I discuss the princess with my reflection.

"She rides like a man, but with a woman's grace. I never thought to try that when I was a woman," says my toad self.

"She hasn't quite perfected the art yet," adds my reflection. "But the long journey back home will see to that."

"It will. With this journey and the one to free her prince, she'll have learned a good many things about surviving in the wild. Even more than I learned in my first time in the forest."

"And then there are the years as wife and mother and queen."

"Yes. Her growth from ignorant child to strong queen hasn't finished yet, but one day she'll be truly amazing."

"You're beating about the bush here. You're avoiding facing what you've seen today."

"I am?"

"Yes. You knew she was a brave, loyal girl when she made her way to you, searching for her lost love. But what does it tell us, that she came back? That she sees you for who you truly are? That she's discerned that you weren't always a toad? That she wants to help *you.*"

My reflection and I are silent, pondering this. To face the truth, that she is the One, the woman who will take on my role when she is old enough and wise enough, means to face other truths as well. That, despite my immense age—my woman years and my toad years combined—I am not immortal. And that the Princess will not always live in comfort, with her family around her and a lovely reflection in her mirror. What sort of wise woman will she be? An ugly crone, like the one that told me the way to save my brothers? A toad, like me? Something even more repellent?

But the power that decrees there will always be wise women to help the young will not take her yet, not while her children are small and her husband is alive. She has many years to enjoy their love and their laughter, all the while growing in wisdom and strength.

In the early years of me being a toad, I knew that not one of the girls who came to my door would be my successor. I had a hundred years of service allotted to me, and I'd outlive them all. But as I passed my half century, I started to eye them and wonder. Which one of these women—some of them barely more than children—was destined to be the next helper? Which one, when her heart's desire had breathed one last breath, when her children's children were grown, would be asked to leave court and company for a two-roomed cabin under dripping trees?

I think I can read it in their faces. Each one beams with love and desire, but none—until now—showed that rare ability to read another's story in her eyes.

I am saddened to think of her leaving so much behind. And yet I know this is foolishness, because when it was time for me to do the same, I did it gladly. I'd known much love. Not in my marriage, though my husband showered gifts on me for the rest of his life, to assuage his guilt. How could I find joy with the man who believed the lies his mother told of me? In our children, yes—they were doubly precious because I'd lost them to the old queen, then won them back again. But the purest, deepest joy I knew was in the company of my brothers, loved all the more for the pain I went through to make their nettle shirts and free them from their enchantment. Yet when my children no longer needed me, and death meant my brother's souls took flight, one by one, I yearned for a new life.

My friends were happy to knit socks by the fire, its light making a halo of their beautiful white hair. For me, though, it was time to return to the forest, my silence this time of my own choosing, to be broken when the moment required it. I hunted out the cottage where I'd first found my brothers, hiding from the cruelty of our step-mother.

I'd expected it to be damp and derelict. I hadn't expected to see smoke rising from the chimney, or the garden brim with roses, half-blown, their petals drifting back to the mulchy earth. I knocked on the door that I'd thought would be mine now.

An old woman opened it. She swam before my eyes. Not because I felt faint or concerned, but because at that moment a different image flitted across her face, a much younger one. I'd seen both these faces before, the youthful one and the old one, though the lines on the latter had deepened over the years.

"Can I help you, dear? I can hardly see these days, but my hearing is good enough." Indeed, now I looked, I could see a milky haze over each pupil.

"Madam, it's you, isn't it? The Fairy Morgana who guided me in the woods? Who told me later, in my dream, how to release my brothers?"

The old woman tilted her head as if to make sure every syllable tipped into her ear, and considered. "Swans, were they?"

"Yes."

"Then you must be Elise! But—if you've come back, that

means…" She halted.

I wondered what stopped her from finishing the sentence.

"Well, well. I mustn't get ahead of myself. Come in, the kettle's on."

I'd not seen much of the cottage when my brothers lived here, only the night I'd found them, when my dream taught me how to break the spell. To do so, I had to sew them each a nettle shirt, in solitude and silence, hidden in the fork of a big old oak tree. Now, the cottage was both familiar and different. The same generous hearth and uneven stone floor, but where drinking horns and pipes had lain scattered over half the surfaces, today the shelves were neatly arranged with cups, saucers and plates, printed with sweet pea and ivy, or that blue willow-pattern which tells an old story of loved ones parted.

"Now tell me why you've called." Madam Morgana carefully angled the kettle to tip the hot water into a teapot.

I hesitated, but one doesn't hide the truth from fairies. "I'd expected the cottage to be empty, Madam. I'd meant to move here for my old age."

"Call me Grandmother, please. I'm far too crooked for Madam these days. You thought the cottage belonged to your brothers, did you? You didn't think to ask them who they rented it off? No, of course, you weren't allowed to speak."

"But where did you live when they had the cottage, Grandmother?"

She waved a hand. "Here and there. You can find many places to hide in the woods if you aren't too precious about it. Hollow trunks, caves worn under the roots of trees by the river. Don't worry, dear, I'm not expecting you to do that. You can stay here, if you wish."

There was an odd look on her face. I tried to read it. Not reluctance, exactly. More as if she thought the reason I'd given for coming was a lie. But I was telling the truth.

"That's very kind of you, Grandmother."

"What do you plan to do with your retirement? Have you brought knitting? If you mean to read, I hope you have your own books. I let the mice nest in mine once my sight began to go."

"I don't know." I felt foolish not having thought this through. "I just longed to remember my brothers. I don't think I meant to sit here being melancholy. I felt that once I was here, I'd know what I was meant to do next."

"Ah." It was like an exhalation. "Yes. I think you will. Take your time, dear."

Madam Morgana was patient. That must have been hard over the next six months, as she saw her own health failing. But it paid off, because when she couldn't get out of bed one morning, and I sat to watch her eat the toast I brought her, I realised I'd come to take on her role. That she hadn't persuaded me, but that I wanted to be the next guide—the fairy godmother, as the young people called her now.

In Madam Morgana's last three days, we discussed the handover. We disagreed on the form I should take.

"A toad?" Madam Morgana gasped at my suggestion, then broke into a coughing fit.

When she'd recovered and I'd wiped the tears from her cheeks, she took up her protest. "A pretty girl like you! What a waste and a shame."

"My looks are faded, Grandmother. A sweet old lady, that's what I see in the mirror."

"And what's wrong with that?"

"Sweet and mild is what made the king pause when he passed me by in the forest. If I'd been ugly and fierce, he'd have left me be, and his mother would never have made me suffer as she did. I want a face that makes lazy, selfish girls take one look and decide they won't trouble me for help after all. And if I'm to return to the forest, I don't want the sunburn and scratches and stings I put up with before. I want a body that will revel in a life in the woods—stones to hide under, worms and slugs to slurp, sun to bask in."

"Why do you want to chase away the lazy girls so soon?" argued

Madam Morgana. "Yes, you have to suffer a few days of them thumping around the house, smashing your crockery, staining your washing, and claiming they're 'cleaning.' But I tell you, it's worth it to see their faces at the end, showered with mud instead of gold!" She broke into a whispery chuckle. "Just make sure they're outside when you do it, not in the parlor."

Madam Morgana said very little after that, and soon slipped into sleep. She dozed off and on for the next few days, and one morning she never woke up. I buried her under her apple tree.

An unfamiliar pain gripped my heart. It took me a week to recognise it for grief. It was a different sorrow from the one that parted me from my brothers. I was mourning the love of a mother. I'd never known the woman who died giving birth to me. My step-mother had driven away both me and my brothers, and my mother-in-law had tried to have me put to death. This woman, who was no relation of mine, had given me the love and guidance I'd had from no one else. And now I knew that this was why I'd come: because it was a wonderful thing she'd done, for me and many others, and I wanted to carry on the work.

Over the years, I've seen a good many young women on the path to their hearts' desire, and a few to their just desserts. Girls whose lovers had forgotten them through enchantment, girls who'd lost their brothers and meant to bring them back, girls who'd lost their men through their own foolish acts, girls who simply wanted the good fortune of their sisters—though only a few stayed on, stubbornly, after they'd seen my face!

More will come. But one day—about forty years from now—an old woman will appear on my doorstep, her dark hair turned bright white, but just as wayward. Will she know then why she's back, or will it take her time, like it did me? Either way, I'll be able to hand my role over to her with an untroubled mind, knowing her big heart will make her the greatest helper of us all. And to think I'd been annoyed at having to delay my nap!

It must be noon now. I hop back to my stone, smooth and cool and dark, and inch underneath. In the blessed damp, my mind at rest, I close my eyes and drift off to sleep.

***

**Lynden Wade** is inspired by history, legends and folklore. She has stories in various publications, including *Enchanted Conversation* and *The Forgotten and the Fantastical* anthology series. She lives in the east of England. Find her on lyndenwadeauthor.weebly.com or on Instagram.

# MY LAST CURSE
Elise Forier Edie

The child would be sweet as a morning sky, with hair like a raven's wing. She would be sharp as a needle and bright as a new-minted coin. She would meet each challenge with the courage of a lion. And she would have the grace of mist tendrils.

Wait. Mist tendrils?

At that, everyone in the throne room gave a little start of surprise. Lords and ladies whispered. A frown crossed the queen's avid features. Only the infant being christened cooed, as her tenth fairy godmother, my sister Lobelia, glided away in a cloud of lavender sparkles.

My sister Rose cleared her throat and swept up to the cradle. "And not only mist tendrils," she declared. "The child will also have the honor and honesty of an angel." Everyone sighed with relief. The hitch in our proceedings smoothed.

"Mist?" I hissed to Lobelia, as she joined me in my hiding place behind a tapestry.

"Well, have you ever really looked at it? It's nicer than you think." Lobelia's purple eyes were wide open but unfocused as usual. "It softens everything beautifully."

Softens, indeed! I shook my head. Lobelia's gifts could be quite stupid at times. She once made a princess "quiet as a snowfall," and the poor girl's voice was never heard. It thwarted all of our plans. Still, "mist tendrils" sounded reasonably harmless.

Rose squeezed in beside us and raised her pink eyebrows. It was almost time for my grand entrance. I had thought long and hard about my curse. I had written down the wording dozens of times. I had taken each draft to my sisters for critique. This time, we were certain we would not fail.

I turned my attention back to the infant as golden-haired Tulip bestowed the second-to-the-last gift ("an artist's eye, she will see beauty in everything"). Then it was my cue. Lightning flashed. The air darkened. I surged out of my hiding place accompanied by a roiling carpet of storm clouds.

"What's this?" I cried in a loud voice, waving a midnight black wand in the air. "Why was I not invited to this party?"

\*\*\*

After the pomp and circumstance, my sisters and I retired for drinks on the back porch of our palace in fairyland. The sun was just setting over twining trees in a blaze of glorious orange and pink.

"A lovely ceremony," Lobelia murmured. "One of our best."

"I thought the lightning flashes were particularly startling." Tulip patted my shoulder.

"But did we do enough?" Rose wondered. "Will we really succeed this time?"

"Yes." I picked up my glass, toasting the sunset. "This curse is perfect. For if no sunlight can touch our princess, no prince can see her. If no prince can see her, none will marry her. And if no prince marries her, she will become queen and finally one of our girls will rule."

"Hear, hear! To the queen!"

"To the Patriarchy toppling!"

"Oh, my dears." Tulip fairly danced, as she raised her glass. "I cannot wait for our girl to be crowned."

\*\*\*

My sisters of course gave every indication they were protecting the princess from my curse. Overnight, a windowless palace sprung up. A clever doorway led underground, so no sunlight would enter the premises. Brilliant tapers burned in the walls, keeping everything bright and warm. Rose and Tulip signed on as permanent nannies and tended our princess lovingly. She grew into everything we could hope for. She was smart. She was funny. She was sweet as spun sugar. Her artist's eye saw beauty, and her busy fingers made it. She spoke ten languages. She added sums in her head. She laughed at danger and loved with passion. She was a credit to us all, in every way. How we adored her.

If only the queen, her mother, had been quiet as a snowfall, we might have had a chance. But the damnable woman would not shut up. And every word she spoke was another nail in a familiar coffin. It had been built and designed by the Patriarchy long ago, to punish and imprison clever girls forever.

"When you are Married," the queen prattled. "When your Prince Comes," she sang. "Your Esteemed Future Husband Whom You Long For," she intoned again and again, and I swear, we could all hear the capital letters in her speech. Even the child's name, Desiree, was a tribute to the queen's sole aim, to wallow in the Patriarchy and then drown her child in its lies.

"She named her the 'Desired One,'" Rose fumed one day. We had shrunk ourselves and taken refuge in the palace wine cellar. There, we could all sit on a bottleneck, like birds on a branch. Rose combed her pink locks and Tulip's golden teeth nibbled on a biscuit. I crouched, as befits an angry blue crab fairy, and picked at a discarded cork with my claws. "As if the poor girl were nothing but a reflection of everyone else's wishes. As if she had no other reason to live than to be desired. A pox on the queen!"

"There is not a teacher or fairy godmother in the world who hasn't wished she could kill the parents of a deeply gifted child," Tulip said.

"But so help me, if we fail again because of this girl's mother, I'll steal my next princess," Rose declared. "I'll hide her away from her parents in a tower, and no one will know who she is. Perhaps then she will truly reach her full potential."

"As for myself," Tulip said. "I will disguise my next princess as a goose girl, so no one considers marrying her. Then she will attain the throne unencumbered and help the poor with real knowledge and purpose."

"For heaven's sake! You're talking like we've already lost this one. We can't give up on Desiree," I said. "Her mother might be an idiot, but the child certainly is not."

Still, it did seem more and more hopeless as time passed. Even living in the dark, our Desiree began to wonder if she was "pretty enough." She worried about the arch of her eyebrows and fretted over her thighs. And we knew for sure all our schemes might fail when, as the child's fifteenth birthday neared, the queen commissioned her portrait to be painted. The plan was to send the picture to all the princes in neighboring kingdoms, so they could look over Desiree and decide if they wanted to mate. Throughout the portrait sitting, the queen hovered and coached the girl. "Stick your chest out, darling!" "Look fierce!" "For God's sake, suck in your stomach." It was maddening. Twice, Rose had to physically restrain Tulip, who growled from a corner of the room like a tiny, golden tiger.

"The girl is fourteen years old. She doesn't need a girdle. She doesn't need a fall in her hair. No diamond choker in the world is as bright as she." Tulip fumed. "Dammit, she looks like a harlot in that picture. Oh, please let me kill the queen."

But Rose wouldn't allow it, for the queen had the right. The profane portraits were dispatched to every prince in the vicinity. Naturally, every single prince sent back their own portrait, along with a proposal of marriage, for what man can resist a fourteen-year-old harlot? The queen practically purred with joy. She had all the princes' pictures hung along a corridor. Then she bade Desiree walk with her while they scrutinized each.

"Pudgy. Absolutely not! Spectacles? Not for you, my girl. That one's too effeminate. That one's too proud." The queen rejected portrait after portrait, to our delight, while Desiree glided by her side, graceful as mist tendrils.

"Speak up! Speak up!" Tulip muttered. "Tell your mother to stop. Tell her you're too young!" She was plodding behind Rose, her face creased with dislike.

"Desiree won't embarrass the queen with an outburst. Don't you remember our sister Lily made the girl as discreet as a whisper? But have no fear! Desiree's better than all of those princes." Rose was serene. "She'll reject every single one."

Alas, Rose had underestimated the queen. So had we all.

"Oh, here now! Look how handsome he is!" They had reached the end of the line and stood before the last portrait. The queen waved her taper and it flickered in the dark. "He is the most perfect model of a man, is he not? What a chin. What a brow. Don't you think, Desiree?"

"I do, Mother." The girl's eyes were bright.

"No, no." Tulip looked alarmed. Rose's face tightened. From my hiding place, I had to stop myself from yelling, "You don't mean it!"

"Do you feel It?" The queen's face glowed with triumph. "Are you experiencing the Most Glorious Moment in a Young Girls' Life?"

"Oh, Mother!" Desiree was certainly feeling something. She fairly thrummed. "Yes! Can this be … Love at First Sight!"

"Darling!" The queen clasped her hands. "He must be the One You Want to Marry!"

"Oh, Mother! It's wonderful!"

There was a thump. Tulip had fallen to the floor. The sheer disappointment had made her faint with rage.

\*\*\*

We retired to fairyland, where it was beautiful as a symphony and always summer. There, while a bevy of gazelle-shaped clouds floated on the horizon, we invoked our sister Jasmin and begged her to investigate Desiree's chosen prince. Jasmin set up a magic mirror. She look deep within it. When the news came, it was even more devastating than we could imagine.

"The five words that best describe him are 'brat,' 'dunce,' 'pig,' 'ass, 'and 'bro,'" Jasmine reported.

"He's an ass and a pig? *Both?*"

"*Plus*, a dunce and a brat?"

"And a bro of the first water. In short, he's a paragon of the Patriarchy." Jasmin squinted at the mirror. "He has a shelf of trophies he didn't earn. He's never worked a day in his life. He throws tantrums about the most trivial of slights. He's all self-esteem with no substance. Plus, he's a racist, a rapist and a rat fink." She clouded up the mirror with a wave of her hand. "And because he's so handsome, every person in the world fawns over him, so he thinks the sun literally shines out of his posterior." Here Jasmin looked even more grim. "He demanded Desiree come to him immediately, even though she is not yet fifteen and under a curse."

"Wait. He's not fetching her himself?"

"Of course he would risk our girl's life to satisfy his desires."

"The queen *would* like him best, wouldn't she?"

I shouted. "But why does Desiree love him? Sisters! We made sure she was clever enough to avoid this." I was losing my composure. My face was hot. "She was supposed to become a marvelous queen and overthrow the Patriarchy! Where did we go wrong?"

"Maybe darkness was the problem?" Rose's red-lashed eyes blinked away tears as I whirled on her. "Constant seclusion and darkness has kept her away from boys and parties and society. But Desiree's never had any adventures, has she? No lakes to dive in. No horses to ride. Not a single handsome stable lad to ruin her. Honestly, this marriage proposal is the first exciting thing that's happened in her life."

"Why didn't we give her a nice, handsome stable lad?" Jasmin bit her knuckle.

"Because she's fourteen!"

"Better him than a Bro-Prince."

"Bottom line, we've failed again." Tulip shook her head. "Another accomplished, beautiful, clever woman, wed at fifteen, enslaved to a numbskull, bound and silenced forever by marriage. And the Patriarchy marches on. Those bastards." Her discouragement was palpable.

But why shouldn't it be? We godmothers had been fighting the Patriarchy for millennia, ever since its invention, when poor Eve first decided an intellect would be an asset. Furious that she had made herself smarter and more creative than Adam, the godfathers quickly invented the Patriarchy, fixing it so women had no purpose but marriage. Under their insidious spells, even Eve's fine mind dulled with drudgery. Plus, every invention she devised was overlooked, every daughter she bore was squashed into obscurity, and every heroine she helped was promptly forgotten or ridiculed. In retaliation, we godmothers showered every princess we could find with a dozen gifts and one careful curse, all crafted in the hopes that just one poor girl might ascend a throne and rule. But the damnable system grew stronger with every year. Our lovely charges always withered in seclusion, while men ran rampant, destroying everything they touched.

Jasmin rallied. "Fontana, there must be a crack in your curse. Drag it out again. I'm sure we left a loophole."

I waved my wand. The curse appeared before us in letters of green and violet smoke. I read aloud. "If she is permitted to see but one ray of daylight, she will rue it bitterly, and it may perhaps cost her her life."

"I let that "her her" go?" Jasmin frowned. "Very bad editing."

"You were tired. It was right after that enchanted sleep failure."

"Oh, damnation." Jasmin swallowed the memory with effort. Then she cocked her white head, gazing at the curse's words as they dissipated in a perfumed breeze. "Well. It's definitely vague enough to work with."

"But Jazz, we don't want Desiree to rue."

"We don't want her to 'pay with her her life,' either."

"She only 'may' pay with 'her her life.' It's not definite. And anyway, just by marrying this idiot, Desiree's bound to 'rue.' So, let's give her a better rue, shall we? Sisters!" Jasmin shook her fist. "We made sure our girl was brave and resourceful and smart. Let's give her a chance to change her fate, and the world's."

Well, put that way, what else could we do? We tried to come up with a plan.

\*\*\*

With Desiree successfully betrothed, the queen's work was done. She retired to her parlor to gloat and left our princess to make travel arrangements herself. Of course, Desiree was quite up to the task. A windowless carriage was prepared for her transport. She ordered that it travel to the Bro-Prince's palace by day, and stop at night, so she could alight after sunset. In this way, every precaution was taken to keep away the curse.

But it was a simple matter to find a disgruntled handmaiden. In a hierarchical society like the Patriarchy, there's always a disgruntled some-girl-or-other. This one was named Cerisette. Rose buzzed near the sleeping girl's ear one night and whispered a little idea. Next morning Cerisette awoke, burning to marry the Bro-Prince herself. Rose helpfully left a knife on the night table, so when Cerisette swung her legs to the floor, she snatched up the weapon, ready to do a mutinous deed.

Thus the royal party departed, Desiree closeted in her windowless carriage, attended by Tulip, Rose and the wicked Cerisette. Tulip festooned the darkness with lights that floated like soap bubbles. Rose sang the soothing songs of fairyland. Distracted by magic, Desiree never noticed Cerisette hacking a hole in the side of the carriage. When honey-colored sunshine streamed in the darkness, I pounced and enacted my curse. The moment sunlight touched her skin, the princess transformed into the prettiest doe, white as a star. Terrified, surprised beyond reason, she bounded into the woods. Tulip, disguised as a butterfly, swiftly pursued.

Selfish Cerisette lost no time. With Rose's help, she patched up the carriage's hole, squeezed herself in one of Desiree's gowns, and shadowed her face with a showy hood, fully prepared to masquerade as the Bro-prince's intended. Feeling quite satisfied, we all wished her luck and hoped their marriage would be a happy one.

"Take that, Patriarchy," I crowed, as the carriage rattled on the wooded path and disappeared around a corner.

***

We knew from experience Desiree's first few hours as an enchanted doe would be the most perilous. She had never experienced light, forests, animals, even plants. Tulip followed her anxiously as she bounded through the trees, startled by everything she beheld. The poor girl could take no real pleasure in her freedom. She could only run blind.

But at last, the white doe tired and stopped by a stream. Her silvery flanks heaved with panic. Her dark eyes rolled in her head. But Desiree looked about with wonder too, beholding for the first time a sun-dappled forest floor, old growth trees soaring. The brook babbled and sang. Smells of earth and flowers wafted. Tulip alighted on a leaf to rest her golden wings, and Desiree plunged her face in the cool water to drink.

"It is lovely, is it not?" I said from my place by the water.

The doe flinched at the sound of my voice. Then she spied me near a flat rock. "What manner of beast are you?"

"I am a crab." I clicked my claws.

Desiree lowered her head to look at me and spied her reflection in the water. She quivered. "What have I become?"

"You are a white doe."

"Oh, rue!" She wept.

"Tut-tut," I said. "Why, think of the freedoms you can enjoy.

Legs to take you anywhere. Food in all parts of the forest. Look at me. I am bound to this brook. But you are bound by nothing at all."

I waited, hoping that the girl would realize her strength, her perfection, that she would see in an instant no bro-prince could match the glories she possessed.

But it was not to be. Still Desiree's lovely black eyes dripped tears. "No!" She wailed. "For now, I shall not be Married and without a Man to Love Me, what good is all this beauty and freedom?"

"Fool! Don't you see? You don't need a –"

With a sound like distant chimes, Tulip transformed. Desiree left off weeping.

"Nurse Tulip!" she cried. "Are you here with this Crab to bear witness to my sorrow?"

"My dear, I am here to see no harm comes to you," Tulip said with infinite patience. "The wicked curse has come to pass, alas, but you are not alone. I shall help you bear it."

She put her arms around the white doe's beautiful neck and threw a warning glance my way. "She'll never believe you, if you just tell her," she hissed while the little doe sobbed. "Desiree has to figure this out for herself. We must trust the wisdom we tried to give her."

***

Jasmin had prepared a cottage for the enchanted princess. While Tulip led her there, I slipped out of my crab form and went to see how things fared with Rose and Cerisette. I found them at sunset, steps from the prince's palace. Rose and I flapped together in an evening breeze, disguised as pennants on a tent.

"Cerisette is a huge bore," Rose reported in an undertone. "She spent the entire trip redoing her makeup over and over. But she is also determined and ambitious and I have hope the prince will be fooled. How fared things with Desiree?"

I told her of the doe's tears and my near outburst. Rose curled herself with displeasure. "The girl is finally free and she's clamoring for chains? Where did we go wrong with her, Fontana?"

"I know not." I felt like weeping. "But I tell you Rose, if this last curse doesn't work, I'm giving up on humanity. Let the Patriarchy ruin the world."

"But the Patriarchy puts the world in peril. What will happen to our girls without us? And the trees and the seas and the sky?"

"I can't concern myself. Again and again, we pour out our gifts. Again and again, our girls aren't permitted to do anything but pleasure princes. It quite ruins the joy of giving. If Desiree doesn't escape her fate, I'm done with godmothering. I'll just be a crab and scuttle in the sea."

Rose sagged. "It's terribly hard to watch them be cut down over and over, isn't it? When they are all so lovely and full of potential."

\*\*\*

Once long ago, a delegation of fairy godmothers met with the godfathers to see if something could be done about their system. By then, all the godfathers had retreated to a sort of clubhouse, where they smoked cigars, napped and wore dressing gowns all day. They had nothing else to do. Under the Patriarchy, princes, giant killers, soldiers and thieves were able to stab dragons, steal treasure, lie to waitresses, plunder, spoil and despoil without a single obstacle in their path. What did they need fairy godfathers for?

Jasmin said, "Look. This Patriarchy thing has gone on long enough. We must allow our girls more opportunity. Besides, your men are making a complete hash of the world. Where once there was a garden, there is a rapidly expanding desert. Please let our girls have a chance."

But the godfathers scoffed. "Pah," they said. "Unheard of." "Everyone knows girls must suffer." "'In suffering shalt they,' and so on." "Plus, wombs!" They rolled their eyes, patted their stomachs and clinked ice in their whiskey and sodas. "Bottom line, my dears, if the girls were in charge, everything would end in blood and torment."

"It's already ending in blood and torment. And fire and flood, if you hadn't noticed."

"There. You see? No help for it." The godfathers yawned.

And so, we were left to heap more gifts and still more gifts on our girls, in the hopes that someday they would rise above and refuse to shackle themselves. But still, we failed.

***

The house Jasmin made to shelter the white doe sat in the middle of the forest. Lobelia had been inserted inside, disguised as an old woman. It was risky relying on Lobelia of course, for she often forgot our mission, and just ate pancakes and read books by the fire. But we felt this might make her a good jailer. All she had to do was provide food and remain marginally watchful, while Desiree and Tulip took refuge in a pretty room with a warm fire and two beds.

"Now listen to me," Tulip told the white doe, as she settled her by the hearth at twilight. "This form of yours only lasts while it is day. So, come nightfall you will become a young woman again. Isn't that nice?"

The doe blinked miserably and turned her face away.

"Come now, Desiree. This curse won't last forever, so let's just make the most of it while it lasts, shall we?" Tulip coaxed. "Why, think! You can roam the forest free and wild by day. You'll learn woodcraft and animal speech! Won't that be fun? And come evening, you and I can pass the time here cozily, reviewing military history."

"But why learn to be a queen, if I can't have my prince?" Desiree moaned.

Tulip ground her teeth. "Dammit to hell," she muttered. "We should have killed the girl's mother while we had the chance."

Meanwhile, things had not fared well with the Bro-Prince. Dim as he was, he was still not fooled by Cerisette. As soon as he saw her, he flew into a rage.

"Do you take me for a fool? Desiree has breasts much larger than that!" he roared.

As usual, we hadn't thought enough about breasts. Poor, treacherous Cerisette was banished in disgrace. Rose followed to settle the poor girl's fortune. After all, it wasn't Cerisette's fault her rack wasn't up to snuff.

Meanwhile, I ventured into the Bro-Prince's chambers. Godmothers usually had nothing to do with men or boys, but in light of the rejection, I felt bound to interfere. I found him hunched in his bed in near darkness, staring miserably at Desiree's profane portrait. He was every bit as square-jawed and golden haired as rumored, with the requisite broad shoulders and clear skin. Tears soaked his manly cheeks. How I despised him.

"Why, what has brought you so low, your Highness?" I quickly took the form of a lamp lighter and began casting a golden glow everywhere.

He moaned into his silk pillowcase. "My pleasure has been ruined. Why did Desiree forsake me?"

"Well. May I speak frankly?"

"Oh, do. I'm at my wit's end."

I took a deep breath. "It's likely she despised you from the beginning, and that's why she sent an imposter."

"You think so?" His voice cracked.

"Your Highness, look at yourself!" I folded my arms. "You're lying around, crying into your pillow. You're demanding Desiree risk her life to come to you. But what have you done for her? Why shouldn't she find you lacking? Have you anything at all to offer the girl?"

He mentioned his scrotum and offered to show me its merits. I declined. "Well, then. What can I do?" He sniffed.

I pressed my advantage. "Do something marvelous. Dangerous! Seek out a strange beast and kill it—a dragon or a sea monster. Then she'll admire you."

"Yes! You're right." He stood. "Fetch someone to dress me. I'm going to make Desiree proud."

Wonderful! I left his room, wishing him the best and hoping he would die.

\*\*\*

Meanwhile, Tulip worked diligently on Desiree both night and day, while Lobelia contentedly lay in a hammock and whiled away the hours. Jasmin's cottage decayed rapidly under her supervision. Mice cavorted in the walls. A family of raccoons moved into the kitchen. Cockroaches swarmed in the sink. But Desiree had been raised in darkness and didn't mind a little dirt. She learned to run and jump. She spent hours outside observing insects, plants and animals. She ceased to think of the Bro-Prince, and she read books, pondered philosophy, and marveled at the stars.

"How perfect the universe is," Desiree said one night while Tulip combed her hair, and the raccoons helped themselves to pancake crumbs from the table, chittering and washing their food in the teapot. "How beautifully all the elements work together. Sun, water, plants, animals. The trees! Have you noticed how wise and generous they are? They help each other to grow and thrive. And the ants, with their endless industry! Such a lesson to be learned in their cooperation. Why don't people work together for the good of all?"

Oh, how pride swelled our bosoms. The next morning, when we sent Desiree off into the forest to gambol, her silvery doe-form slipping amongst the tree trunks, Jasmin declared, "Another month in the woods and we will make her a queen to be reckoned with. This curse has fulfilled all my fondest hopes, Fontana. I believe we did it. The Patriarchy is toast."

"Indeed, we have them by the gonads." I smiled.

Of course, that was the same morning the Bro-Prince shot our white doe with an arrow and she fell, even as we were crowing with triumph.

\*\*\*

"Thank goodness he's a terrible archer." Tulip shivered a little later. "Or the prince might have killed Desiree."

By then, it was night. We had shoved Desiree in the cottage and bade Lobelia nurse her injuries. Then we retired to the yard, where it smelled less of raccoon scat and more of moss and flowers.

"He's hobbled her. Pierced her leg!" Jasmin seethed. "Could he not behold a pretty white doe without shooting it? Doesn't he know a doe should not be killed at all?"

"What I want to determine," said Rose, who had only just returned from setting up poor Cerisette in a profitable business, "Is why did the prince venture into the woods in the first place? I was under the impression all he ever did was drink beer and crush the cans on his head."

That's when I had to say, "Oh, dear."

The others looked at me. "What did you do, Fontana?" Jasmin demanded.

***

They were furious, but it didn't matter, for I was more furious with myself.

"You *told* him to shoot a strange beast?"

"I thought he'd fall off a cliff or be eaten by an ogre. Honestly, I just wanted him to die." I was sobbing so hard with remorse, I could scarcely speak. "I'm sorry! Truly I am," I cried. "But perhaps we can salvage this? The prince didn't kill her. And he won't find her in the forest. The arrow wound might make even Desiree hate him! Sisters, this could still come out all right. Couldn't it?"

But just then, Lobelia called from the cottage. "Oh, my darlings!" Her vapid face was unaccountably bright in the moonlight. "Do come see what came in from the wood." She delivered the deathblow with a saucy grin. "I couldn't help inviting him in. He's as handsome as a god."

A tiny crash echoed through the forest, as poor Tulip fainted again with rage.

***

After that, there was absolutely no hope. Upon beholding his manly form, Desiree forgave the Bro-Prince immediately.

"How could you help but try to shoot me, my dearest?" she cried and threw herself into his arms.

There was nothing left to do but to lift the curse immediately and send them off to be wed. Poor Desiree was still limping, but her lovely face shone with joy.

"It's my fault. I gave her the honor of an angel," Rose said. "She couldn't forsake her promise to him."

"It's my fault. I made her see beauty in everything," Tulip said. "She saw beauty in his faults and forgave him."

"It's my fault. I didn't proof the curse well enough," Jasmin said. "We should have made Desiree's betrothed die, if she saw sunlight."

"Well, it wasn't my fault." Lobelia said. "I just gave her the grace of mist tendrils and it harmed nothing."

For once, Lobelia was right. And anyway, we all knew it was all my fault. I had all but sent the prince into Desiree's arms. On the day of her nuptials, I went into the sea forever. Life as a crab is brutish and violent, but at least I don't have to watch any more lovely, clever princesses sold into wedlock and slavery.

Sometimes, one of my sisters visits. They tell me everything's much the same in the world, for the Patriarchy still has the strength of diamonds and tears.

"And it's such a faulty system!" Jasmin railed, the last time I saw her. "Why do humans keep putting their faith in it?"

"The godfathers won't stand for anything else. And neither will the men."

"What we need is a champion." Her eyes blazed. "A girl warrior, not a princess, who will save a country, and end a hundred years war. If we can achieve that, the Patriarchy will have to let women rule. Won't they?"

I heard from Rose, they burned that poor child for a witch.

Rose told me too that lately even our stories have changed. Now, the godmothers don't even battle the godfathers. Instead, they exist only to help lonely princesses find love.

"All the stories make us fat and silly. We fix girls up with pretty gowns and glass slippers that dissolve at midnight."

"What? Why?"

"So they can meet men incapable of making up their minds." Rose sighed. "That's the role of a fairy godmother now."

"Really?"

"History is written by the victorious," Rose said. "I'm finally following your example, Fontana, and retiring to a hot house." And that's what Rose did.

Only Lobelia ever truly lifts my spirits when she visits. Perhaps she is the wisest of us, after all. Just last week, she cozied up to my hole and said, "How beautiful the Patriarchy has made our oceans. See at how the sunlight filters through the water and lights up all the bits of plastic floating in it? It's rather like stained glass, don't you think?"

"Stained glass with the grace of mist tendrils," I said.

"Yes!" Lobelia laughed. She danced in the murky water, beautiful as a dream. "Oh, sister. Isn't it wonderful? How glad I am that we are together to see it."

***

**Elise Forier Edie** is an author and scriptwriter based in Los Angeles. Her fantastic fiction has appeared in anthologies and magazines, most recently in *Water: Selkies, Sirens and Sea Monsters*, edited by Rhonda Parrish, and in *Mysterion Magazine*. You can learn more about her at her website eliseforieredie.com.

# FACE IN THE MIRROR
Sonni de Soto

It all started out so simple. You see a grown prince, one bad dragon slaying or territory war away from the throne, being a royally entitled brat... well, what's a magical being to do?

As a fairy, there was really only one thing *to* do: I put one small, tiny, little spell on him. It was one of those heat of the moment kind of things that just comes out when tempers rise.

Maybe it wasn't my finest moment, but I honestly never thought it would spiral this badly.

I spy through the mirror in my room and frown, when I see him reflected through his own mirror in his bedroom. I shake my head as the prince prowls the floor like the trapped beast my spell transformed him into. He's not quite on all fours—yet—but he's hunched over as he stalks the room. Still dressed in the tatters of the fine clothes he'd worn to the party, he looks a mess. Tufts of dark fur peek out of ripped seams. His boots had been completely destroyed in the transformation, leaving him barefoot to pace about on high-arched, long-toed, padded paw-like feet. His face, now a magically mangled mix of man, lion, wolf, and bull, wears an expression as monstrous as its form. And his angry mutterings sound like a half language, an animalistic take on speech.

He's in one of his rages. I stiffen as I listen to him rend curtains and smash furniture. I cough to get his attention. "Do you really think this is productive?"

He growls, the sound low and menacing, before pouncing in front of the mirror. His lips curl to reveal sharp, pointed teeth. The mirror begins to fog with his hot breath as his snout wrinkles and his nostrils flare. Even the fur covering him seems to stand on end with his fury, making him look even larger. I can see his claws at the edge of the glass as he clutches the frame.

But it's his ice blue eyes—still human and so full of anger—that scare me the most. "I don't want to hear anything from you, witch." He sneers. "You did this to me. Undo it. Now."

I roll my eyes. "I can't." We've been over this before. "I cast the spell, but you're the only one who can break it."

"And, I told you, I can't." He begins to pace again over the now scratched floors and rugs in front of the mirror in frustration. "*Beast you act, so beast you'll be. Till gifted love shall set you free. Find one you care for, and who does so back. Or your normal form, you'll forever lack.*" He snorts as he shakes his foot when one of his claws snags on the rug. "What utter nonsense."

My spine stiffens. Okay, it hadn't been my most eloquent spell. "Well, it worked, didn't it?"

He kicks the rug across the room. "It certainly did." He huffs and glares at me. "So well it scared every living soul out of the palace, from the guests to the servants." He sits down on the now bare floor with a sad sigh. "To my own parents."

I wince again. Yeah, I hadn't seen that coming.

All night, I'd seen him be rude and snap at every person he came into contact with. He'd thrown food back at servants for being too hot or too cold. He'd berated and disrespected his knights, finding nothing but fault in their duties. And he'd yawned at and dismissed dignitaries and guests as beneath him.

But, yes, I'll admit what had sealed both our fates was seeing how he treated the ladies at the party. He would swagger up to them and act as if it ought to be their great privilege to speak to him. As if he expected them to fawn over him, only to mock those who did and resent those who wouldn't. He'd spent most of the night judging them callously, often to their faces, as too fat or too thin or homely or overly made-up. He'd even brought one poor girl to tears.

Then he'd approached me. Telling me that I was far too old and had much too plain a face for my dress, but that he supposed he could dance with me anyway.

I'd been so angry, the spell had just boiled over, seething out of me like scorching steam.

In truth, I never meant for the spell to last so long. *Find one you care for, and who does so back* shouldn't have been so difficult. It's not as if I was asking for *true love*—whatever that means—or even romantic love. Just any kind of love. I figured the prince would have his snit, calm down, then his parents or a friend would sit him down and have a talk with him about his inappropriate behavior. Everyone would hug and—poof—the whole ordeal would be over in, like, two hours.

But then they'd all run from him. Every one of them had fled. Leaving him all alone in this empty castle for days now.

"They're never coming back, are they?" His voice is so quiet I can barely hear it, but I feel each word like a stab to my heart. "None of them."

I'd just wanted to teach him a lesson to not take the people around him and the position he held for granted. I just wanted him to see that he was hurting those around him, most of whom were just trying to take care of him and his future kingdom.

Instead, he learned how little anyone actually cared.

Guilt pricks at me as I worry my lip.

I shake my head. This isn't my fault.

It isn't.

How could I have known a little fur and fangs would terrify

everyone so? For goodness sake, the kingdom to the north had their prince turned into a frog last year and the one to the south has half a dozen or so swans sitting on their thrones. I didn't think this place was so squeamish about such things.

"I'm hungry."

I look up at him, sitting alone on the floor in the middle of his room in the empty royal estate. He sounds so helpless.

I shake my head. No, I will not feel sorry for him. He is a grown man. A future king. And now, after my spell, a rather intimidating monster. He is many things, but *helpless* is not—or at least should not—be one of them. "When was the last time you ate?"

His shoulders hunch in on themselves, making his hulking form as small as possible. "Yesterday morning. I finished the last of the food in the dining hall."

Stale party leftovers more than a day ago. Well, no wonder he's so cranky. "Well, then get yourself something from the kitchen."

He shoots me a disbelieving look. "By myself?"

Well, yes. "Unless you have a better idea."

He shifts his weight from side to side. "I've never cooked before. I don't know how."

Unsurprising, since he grew up in a palace with servants to attend his every whim and want. "I would suggest a sandwich." Even a pampered prince could manage to put meat and cheese between two slices of bread. "You should be able to handle that on your own."

He bristles, his spine shooting straight up with indignation. "Of course, I can. I'm not a child."

Then why do I feel like his mother? "Good. Let me know if you have any trouble."

***

I was surprised when, after an hour, he came back with half a chicken breast and an unevenly cut hunk of cheese between two smushed slices of bread. It looked sloppy, but the expression on his face had been priceless.

It was the first meal he'd ever prepared himself and I watched him eat it as if it were a favored gourmet delicacy.

And then who'd have thought he would wake me up this morning, pounding on the mirror to show me the breakfast of burnt eggs and bacon he'd made?

Thankful the magical mirror transmits images and not smells, I give him a tense smile. "Looks great." His fur is singed in places and a cut on his finger has been hastily bandaged with some torn cloth, but he has the biggest grin on his face and his shoulders are held high with pride.

He nods. "It took a little doing to figure out the stove, but I did it."

I study the plate again. I suppose he did. And that actually is quite the accomplishment. "Well, bon appétit." I smile back at him before he begins to dig into his meal.

"By the way," the prince says between bites, "I wanted to talk to you about this whole curse-business."

I look up at him. "What about it?"

He chews a few more times before swallowing. "Let's look at this line by line." He licks his lips. "*Beast you act, so beast you'll be.*"

I snort. Well, that one was easy enough to figure out.

He coughs pointedly. "*Till gifted love shall set you free.*" Still pouting slightly, he tilts his head thoughtfully. "Gifted love." He taps his fork against the table. "I need someone to give me love."

I frown as flecks of food fly off the fork, speckling the mirrored glass and table with bits of yolk. I'm so glad I'm not actually in that room with him.

"Easy!" He stands up and begins to pace. "I'll find some woman and pay her to marry me. Marriage vows, they're the quintessential symbol of love being given. It's perfect." He slaps his hands together conclusively. "This whole thing will be done before nightfall."

I shake my head. "That's not love."

He scoffs. "It's marriage." He shakes his own head dismissively.

"That's the culmination of love."

"Not like that, it's not." I shrug. "Paying a woman—any woman—to marry you." I raise a skeptical eyebrow. "That's not love; that's business." I wag a finger at him. "That won't break even the most basic spell."

He growls and sits back down. "Fine, let's keep going. What's the rest?" He kicks his feet up to rest them on the edge of the table, so he can lean back in the chair. Even with the mirror for a magical barrier, I recoil, staring at the bottoms of his feet now covered in dust and grease and who knows what else from the kitchen floors. He taps his foot in the air, thinking. "*Find one you care for, and who does so back. Or your normal form, you'll forever lack.*" He sits up straight again. "What a joke! I have to find someone I care about and somehow get them to care about me too? All while looking like this!" He gestures with his claws at himself. He grunts and tosses his fork across the room. "It *is* a joke. A cruel one."

I wince as I hear the small bit of silver strike the wall and floor. I don't know what to say. Looking at it all now, it does seem... daunting.

His fang worries his lip a bit. "What about a long-distance kind of arrangement?" He ponders more. "Like a pen pal sort of thing. Love letters!" His eyes stare off in thought. "There are princesses in faraway kingdoms. I even know a few desperate for husbands. I could write one of them. Maybe multiple ones. Surely, I can make one of them fall for me that way."

I let out a short laugh before trying to cover it up. "I've seen your form of seduction, remember?" I roll my eyes. "You'll never make someone fall in love with you that way."

He rolls his own eyes. "I wasn't trying to seduce *you*." He puffs up his chest indignantly. "If I was trying to seduce you, you'd be..." his brow furrows as he shrugs and says, his voice losing steam, "seduced." He crosses his arms over his chest. "I could make a woman—any woman—fall in love with me, if I tried." He turns to shoot me a sharp look. "Or at least I could, before you did *this* to me."

Oh, please! "And exactly how many women did you get to fall in love with you before my spell?"

I regret the words the moment I said them. Especially when his face falls. I bite my lip.

I shut my eyes and sigh. "What I mean is: I cast the spell because the way you treat people, especially women, isn't the best way to make people like you, much less love you."

He huffs haughtily. "I'm a prince; what's not to love?"

I choke on a scoff. "Sure, a snobbish slob who looks down his nose at everyone he meets; how could anyone resist?"

I purse my lips together. I did it again. He looks angry, but only in an attempt to hide his embarrassment. Even as his fists clench in ready rage, I can see shame and worry fill his vulnerable eyes. I hold out my hands in peace. "I'm sorry." I take a deep breath. "I just mean that anyone who loves you just because you're a prince doesn't really love you."

He's silent for a long time, just picking at the now cold food on his plate. "Well, then, I guess it's impossible." His claws tap and scrape across the china. "As you pointed out, I clearly have no idea how to make someone love me."

He doesn't get it. That was the point of the spell. "You don't *make* people fall in love with you." It's the lesson he was supposed to learn. "You treat people—all people—the way you want to be treated. Then, along the way, you find special people you want to share your life with and, if they feel the same way, you do your best to live a life worth sharing with them."

With a sad laugh, he shuts his eyes. "I don't even like my life;" he says with a defeated shrug, "why would anyone else want to share it?"

I look at him. He suddenly seems so small in the large, empty room, so miserably alone in this large and lonely place.

This was supposed to be so simple.

I shrug. "Well, maybe you should think of this as a chance for you to make a better life for yourself."

He looks at me in disbelief. "And how do I do that?"

I sit up. "I don't know. But, if I were you, I'd stop worrying about how to make someone fall in love with me." He's a frightening beast in an empty estate; his options for finding someone new to love are not great. "If we're being honest, we have no idea when or how this spell might end." I stop myself from pointing out that it might *never* end. "So, if this is your life for the foreseeable future, you'd be better off thinking of ways to make it one *you* love, right?"

\*\*\*

I don't know what I expected after that conversation. I don't know if he did either. But, day by day, I began to see a change in him. It started out small. I noticed he spent more time in his room, reading books on herbs and cooking. The meals he would bring to eat in front of the mirror would get more and more complex, starting with things like porridge then breads then roasts.

It'd taken him about a month and several trips to the royal library before he began to make food anyone else would eat. He began to learn about technique and style and flavor. Even when the kitchen stores began to run low, he taught himself how to hunt and grow his own food. Nothing fancy, mostly whatever was already running wild in the nearby forest, but still impressive. And, every mealtime, he would bring his latest creation to the mirror and we would dine together.

Tonight, with grand flourish, he lifts the metal serving cloche to reveal rabbit stew with wild roots and greens.

As he takes a mock bow, I clap. "You really have learned so much in so little time."

After laying a napkin over his lap, he begins to eat. "Thank you. But I can't take all the credit. Survival is an exceptional teacher."

I shake my head. He's selling himself short. "You have more than survived." I look at his meal flavored with delicate wild garlic greens and edible wild flowers. For such a simple meal, it looks lovely. Even he looks different now. No longer wearing rags from his old life, he'd scoured the castle for clothes that fit him, dressing himself in an odd mismatch of various servants' clothes. But at least he now keeps both himself and his clothes clean, making perhaps not the most princely of appearances but charming all the same. "You should be proud of yourself."

He gives me a small, wry smirk as he swallows a bite of rabbit. "If only Mother and Father could see me now. I'm sure *pride* could not quite cover their feelings."

The night passes pleasantly enough. A gardener myself, we exchange tips and tricks we've learned. And, again, I'm marveled by how much he's taught himself. Yet a part of me can't stop thinking about that phrase.

I wonder what his family *would* think of him, thriving by himself. Finding passion and joy all his own. Finding fulfillment in watching his hard work reap rewards. He is so different than the boorish, selfish young man I met the night of the party. The transformation is more than I thought possible with my silly, little spell.

I am so proud.

I can't imagine his parents wouldn't be also.

As I listen to his plans to expand his garden, I begin to plot my own idea.

***

Well, this is awkward.

It'd taken some doing and more trips to the neighboring kingdom than I'd expected to get the king and queen to agree to come to the castle for a meal. When I'd finally gotten them to agree, so they could see the changes in their son that I had, I'd told the prince. Who, looking back, hadn't seemed as excited as I'd expected either. Perhaps I should have taken that as a hint.

Well, too late now.

Sitting silently in the castle's dining hall in the middle of this rather awkward reunion, I spoon fragrant soup to my lips, while watching the king and queen sneer at their bowls, and find myself missing my mirror. The queen turns the bowl slightly, looking at the soup as if it might attack her. "So…" Her nose wrinkles a bit. "You made this yourself?"

I nod. "Yes, your son has become quite the chef as of late. He even grew most of the vegetables and caught all the game."

The queen's eyes widen even as her face pales. "He *caught the game*." Without turning to her husband, she says, "Did you hear that, dear, our son *caught* our meal?"

The king lets out a disgusted sound. "Well, of course, he did." He shoves the bowl and plates away from him. "He probably skinned it with his teeth, by the look of him."

The prince stiffens, but says nothing, just continues to eat his meal. His shoulders are hunched and his head bowed. I can't see through all the fur, but I can imagine heated embarrassment flushing his face. "I have rabbit traps in the forest and by my garden and the lake is quite good for fishing." He eats another bite of his meal. "You should know, Father; you used to hunt and fish on the grounds all the time."

The king shifts in his seat indignantly. "For sport. We hunt beasts of the chase—foxes and red deer and the like—for the challenge and thrill of it. Not out of survival, like some…" The king waves his hand, searching for the word.

"Beast?" The prince sits up straight—or as straight as his form will allow. He looms large over the table, so much bigger than the rest of us. "Is that what you were about to say?"

"Well, look at you!" The king pounds his fist on the table, shaking the fragile china. "When we were invited here, we thought it was because you'd finally managed to lift the curse. Only to arrive and find out that you've wasted your time learning to eat weeds and rodents." He pounds his fist again. "This is not how a prince behaves! This is not how a son of mine behaves. In this family, we slay monsters; we do not become them!"

The prince sits up straighter. "What are you saying, Father?"

The king's face flushes as he stands. "I'm saying that I am the king and this is my palace and, if you're just going to live like an animal, you don't deserve it. You might as well live in the forest like one as well." He tugs at his waistcoat. "Before you're dealt with like one."

"Dear!" The queen holds her hand over her chest in shock.

"No, no, I mean it." The king waves his hands in the air. "Either you break this curse immediately or you are no longer welcome in this castle, do you hear me?"

The prince stands as well. "I hear you just fine, Father."

Holding my hands out in a plea for calm, I stand up too. "Wait a minute." This was not how things were supposed to go. "He's your son."

"*That* is not our son." The queen shakes her head wearily. "Not anymore."

The king turns his angry gaze at me. "All because of you and your witchery. If you hadn't cast that spell…"

I meet his gaze right back, feeling my own ire begin to bubble within me. "If you had just loved your son," I point out, "the spell would have been broken the night of the party."

"How dare you?" The queen's face is set in outraged lines. "How dare you try to make us out to be bad parents. Of course, we loved our son." She waves at him. "Before you did *this* to him."

My spine straightens and my hands flex as I feel my magic begin to swirl within me. I can almost taste the bitter spell forming on my tongue.

The prince lays a calming hand on my arm before shoving his chair further back to step away from the table. "If you'd truly loved me, Mother," he says sadly but resignedly, "it shouldn't matter what anyone did to me. Whatever I look like, I am your son, and that should have been enough. If a simple spell could break it, how strong was your love to start with?"

For a long moment, no one says anything. The prince just stares at his parents who suddenly can't meet his gaze. "Excuse me, Mother. Father." He nods to both before leaving.

I look at the two stiff royals still fuming over the untouched food their son had made for them and I suddenly feel nothing but pity for them. They *could* have just loved their son. Not just now. Not just the night of the party. But from the day he was born. But they hadn't. Maybe they'd loved the idea of him. An heir. A future version of them to continue the line. But that wasn't him. That wasn't enough.

And, now that he's learned to love himself enough to leave, it was more their loss than anyone's.

So, I leave as well, following the prince outside. Well, not *the prince*. Not anymore. I wince. Once, again, my simple, little, tiny spell had unintentionally taken one more thing from him. His home. His hope that, one day, it—not just the place itself, but his family, his life, and his position within it—would be his again. I sigh. This is all my fault.

He stops on the steps of the palace and stares down the path leading away from the only home he's known.

I walk up to him. "Are you all right?"

"I'm sorry."

My brow furrows. "For what?" If anything, I'm the one who should be sorry. I'd thought this would be a good idea. Get everyone in the same room and talk things out.

He turns to me. "I'm sorry for the things I said that night." He frowns. "It was rude and uncalled for and I don't think I ever apologized to you. I didn't like myself much then and that made it hard to like anyone else. Made it impossible to imagine anyone liking me." He looks at me thoughtfully. "Strange as it sounds, I'm grateful for your spell. It forced me to think about who I am and who I want to be." He smiles and reaches out his hand to me. "So, truly, I'm sorry and thank you."

I take his hand, his soft fur against my skin such a contrast to the calloused pads of his fingers and palms. He holds my hand tightly but gently, consciously being careful of his claws. I meet his gaze. "I accept your apology and offer one of my own. None of this happened quite as either of us expected and, while I regret so much of what came of my spell, I am glad if you've come out better because of it."

"I became better because of you." He squeezes my hand. "You stayed with me. After everyone else left, you stayed. I will never forget that."

Squeezing his hand back, I stare in wonder as the fur on his hand fades away. The grip of his hand changes as the bones in his fingers and palm shift and his beastly claws shrink away. My gaze meets his in surprise as I watch his posture, body, and face morph, shrinking and reshaping itself. I look on in wonder as he transforms, bit by bit, back into a human.

I cover his hand with mine, his fur-less flesh cool to the touch with the effort and shock of changing. "You did it! You broke the spell."

"We did." He sounds a bit breathless. He blinks a bit, still disbelieving. He stares at our hands before looking up at the palace again.

I pat his now stiff fist. "You could go back." I shrug. "You are a prince again."

He frowns and stares at the grand building with its high towers and gilded walls, with its countless lonely rooms and empty halls. "I don't think I am anymore." Shaking his head, he lets go of my hand and turns away. "It's not a life that made me, or anyone around me, very happy. It's not a life I want to share with anybody."

Thinking of the king and queen, I don't blame him. I shrug. "Well, you're welcome to stay with me, if you like." I'm not entirely sure how that would work, but it feels wrong to leave him on his own.

"Thank you." He looks down the path, leading through the forest and into the village on the other side of the thick trees. "But I think

I'm ready to find my own life somewhere else. Somewhere out there. Maybe as a cook. Or I could find a farm to work on."

I nod, wishing him luck while also knowing he'll do well for himself. "That sounds lovely." When he looks back at the castle and frowns, I ask, "What is it?"

"I left the mirror in my room. I've become so used to having you with me. Watching over me." He turns to me. "How will I ever see you again?"

I smile. "When friends want to see each other, they find a way. I have no doubt we will meet again."

"Friends." He says it as if he's testing the word out on his tongue. He smiles. "Yes, I will make sure of it." And, with that, he nods, bids me farewell, as I watch him head down his new path.

***

**Sonni de Soto** is an author of color, who's had the privilege of publishing novels and stories with Cleis Press, SinCry Publishing, *Speculatively Queer*, and many others. To find more from her, please visit patreon.com/sonnidesoto and instagram.com/sonnidesoto_allages/.

# FORGETFUL FROST
Vivica Reeves

He always remembered… something. Which was odd because he did not remember much. He had been walking alone for so long, and so far, he forgot who he was. He forgot how he came to be. He forgot why he was alone. The little he did know, the call of the frost and death's unchanging selfish ways, did not bring him any comfort. The emptiness of his forgetfulness terrified him. If it did not stop, it would consume him.

Though when he tried to remember, pain and anguish weighed heavily in him. His back hunched over, succumbing to the weight. For a moment, there would be relief as he let his crystal staff support him. That relief would quickly break with a resounding crack from his staff as he fell to the ground. Full of anger, confusion, and hurt, broken on the ground, he would roar. The wind joined him as if it could ease his pain. It only added to the never-ending cold that pierced his skin. He roared, and roared, and roared. The feelings, the pain, did not end.

Until he stopped trying to remember. Then he would be numb to the cutting cold that crawled from him. He would not care about the choked cries that froze around him. The emptiness would be so close to consuming him. Yet, his terror would be gone. Replaced with a weariness that froze him. It dragged him to his knees, the crystal staff in his hands useless and lifeless. Just like the heart in his chest. It was in those times, Spring in her splendor and beauty would shimmer before him.

"Morozko, King of the Frost."

A name he did not remember, but he answered to it. Though he knew it was not his name. Just as he knew the call of frost. Just as he knew that Spring needed him. Just as he knew that he needed her to continue their dance. Whatever his name was before he woke up in frost, he knew not.

"I have need of you."

Name or not, their dance continued. Slowly, his weariness would melt away in her presence. He would give a nod. With sad, familiar bluebell eyes that awakened the nerves in his cold piercing skin, Spring would ask him to go. Go to this village, preserve these plants, then keep going, and he would. He could never refuse her, just as he could never fully forget the pain and that she never stayed. She never came close to him. She would only request his help and leave. It hurt and left him colder than before; still, they would continue their dance.

Things changed when Spring came and walked with him. She stepped close to him. She changed their dance. For there was no need for her at that moment. He could keep walking, the pain of remembering having not broken him yet. Still, here she stood. It was not their dance, their routine. So, he ignored her and listened to the frost's song. Still, she continued with him and waited for his response. He urged the frost to grow colder, making her shiver as she still walked with him.

"Are you warm, dear beauty?"

His voice crackled like the frost that escaped from his staff. Laughter, sharp and tinted with hostility, came from Spring's lips. He only heard pure laughter from the abodes of mortals as they hid from him. It was rare for laughter to be as sharp as Spring's. Those kinds of defiant laughs were made by those who were badly hurt before.

"Whether I am warm or not, is no concern of yours, Morozko. But I have need of you."

As she continued to walk, she told him of a woman who begged for a child in Belarus, a village near him. While it was still Winter, she could not appear to the woman unless life was being birthed or grown. It was he who had to give the woman Spring's blessing. Spring asked him to give the woman a blessed lotus to eat. It would give the woman the child she desired.

"Is it worth it to give life when death will follow?"

Spring cradled the lotus in her hand and brought it to her chest. The anger in her eyes was marred by the subtle deep sorrow that always haunted them.

"It is worth it if life can be loved."

Spring asked once more for him to give the lotus to the woman. Going back into their normal dance, he did not refuse. He took the flower to the woman. The woman was grateful, and truly smiled at him as she consumed the flower. The woman's soft, true smile made him remember something.

A smile of a woman with graying golden hair as she rubbed her stomach. The clarity of the memory and the sudden rush of joy cracked the ice in his chest. He bent over and fell to his knees gasping. Pain beat in his chest, but it did not consume the sudden rush of warmth that came with that single memory. Shocked as he was, he did not see the woman, the soft and true mortal woman, reach out to touch him.

Immediately, when the woman's fingers brushed his clothes, she fell to the floor. Frost nibbled her fingertips as she cried out in pain, waking him from shock. The warmth from before flew away as a new fear gripped him. He ran away like a cowardly mortal, leaving the shivering woman on the doorstep. Guilt made him freeze and look back. His need to right the wrong his cold caused, had him take the frost's song away from the woman. Yet, it was the hope to remember that made him stay at the edge of the woods and watch through Winter's cycle and beyond.

He watched as the woman shakily stood back up. How her husband smiled and held her when he learned of Spring's blessing. They celebrated as the woman still shivered, and she never stopped shivering. To her it was always too cold. No number of woolen blankets could warm her. Even when her husband held her tight, she still shivered. Though, despite her never-ending cold and constant pain, she never lost her smile. She smiled as her husband held her. She smiled as she sang to the life growing within her womb. She smiled as the wind that rattled their fence, in any season, never touched their house.

"Thank you, Morozko."

She smiled at him.

It was all so painfully familiar to him. Instead of the woman's brown hair and brown eyes, he saw graying golden hair and bluebell eyes. His own arms radiated the warmth the husband held in his arms as he cradled his wife. The wind froze the warm water that he did not realize had poured out of him. With every single glimpse at the haunting memories, his heart began to beat and his chest felt warm. Though the pain within him grew heavier and heavier, pinning him to the ground at times, he still remembered.

The woman's stomach grew and her skin became paler. At the beginning of another Winter's cycle, he was still there watching the woman. There was a change in the air as Spring shimmered beside him.

"It is time."

He nodded and the woman let out a cry in pain. Quickly, Spring glided into the house. For this was her domain as the Winter outside was his. Spring disguised herself as a handmaiden, she directed and led them into the process of giving life; she touched them.

He could only clear away the clouds to offer them the light of the full moon. The moon's luminescent light blended into the woman's glistening pale skin and highlighted her lips that were turning blue as she cried. When the woman's lips were darker than any violet flowers he saw, and her breath came out in visible shaky puffs, the cry of a small baby girl was heard. He dared to go to the window, to peek at something he never let himself see before, the breath of life.

Spring, splendid beautiful Spring, cradled the child to her chest and slowly stroked the babe's face with an elegant finger. A shimmer ran down her cheek as her smile wavered. The thumping in his chest increased, shattering the ice within his chest. He buckled forward, leaning on the window. The ice that shattered within him flowed from his body and onto the window, creating a sharp frost he had never seen before.

As the odd frost covered the window, the three beings in the room looked at the window. The husband saw the frost and thought the room was getting colder and so sought a covering to warm the woman from it. This left Spring and the woman looking at him. The woman beckoned Spring to her. With violet-blue lips, she whispered something in Spring's ear and turned to the window, to him. As she smiled still, he felt the warmth of life leave her body from outside the house. In the departing warmth, he heard a whisper.

"Watch over her."

His focus turned back to Spring as she came out of the house, leaving the crying babe in the husband's arms. At the husband's blank face, a shiver ran down his spine. The moment Spring was beside him, he spoke his concerns about the husband.

"He is weak."

"He can change. That is what life does."

Spring stood next to him and smiled hopefully at the babe through the window. He huffed and shook his head. Life seemed to change, but it truly was a cycle. A repetitive change that led to death. He should know, for he saw it end. Even now, when a life was born, another ended. He could not afford to care. The immobilizing pain that came from his heart had now distracted him and caused him to hurt people, twice. He could not let it happen again.

"She asked for us to watch the girl," Spring gently prodded.

"Death cannot watch life. It can only take from it," he stated.

"Do you only know how to walk away and leave ruins?"

He blinked. Spring's hands were clenched and her teeth gritted. Her hair flew around her as if she, and she alone, was suffering from a raging tempest. He looked away, ignoring the way his heart tried to hammer away the ice in his chest.

"Ruins tell you what needs to be taken down and what can be rebuilt."

As soon as he finished speaking, the wind paused and the frost grew quiet, giving birth to the tense silence between him and Spring. Then, in a blink, Spring left. He stood alone at the window, gazing at the blank husband and the crying babe. Frost resumed singing and the wind howled. Still, he did not know what to do. So, he left into the forest, too.

A few days later, he went back to Belarus. Not to watch the babe, but to bring frost back to the village. The doors were closed and warm porridge was left out. Mortals believed he would be appeased by their gifts. But frost was frozen and did not care if it was tended to. Nor did he.

As he went through the village, he heard crying. The sound was distracting. He followed it, wondering if he could freeze the noise so that he could do his work in silence. The noise led him to the house of the woman. The woman who was soft and true. The woman who was consumed by his frost. The woman who asked him to watch her child.

Death did not watch life, but he was not watching. He was trying to silence the sound. The sound coming from the child. The window to the child's room was opened. He looked for the woman's husband. The husband was sitting in a chair, head in his hands, begging for his child, a girl, to be silent. For he was hungry too.

It would be easy to go in and use his frost to freeze both the child and the husband. They could join the woman. They would not be hungry. They could see her smile, as he did when the woman died. Then the child looked at him, and for a moment she stopped crying. For a moment, he saw gold hair and winter-green eyes. He could not take this girl's warmth.

With a crack, he left the house and went back into the village. Using his staff and magic, he collected a few bowls of porridge. Then he took them back to the house, pushing them in with his staff, so he did not have to enter or touch anything. As a parting gift, he even used a breeze to close the girl's window. The girl's cries dimmed and the heavy frost he had laid down began to melt as he sank to the floor outside the cottage. For he remembered that he had always wanted a girl.

He continued not to watch the girl but he made sure she did not distract him. The girl cried for food; he silenced her with his offerings. She cried for warmth; he left the village early. She cried for company; he led a hound to her. She cried in her loneliness; his frost appeared and had a woman, with a child of her own, fall into the husband's arms. He gave her all that he could, but it was not enough. The girl was still a distraction, a hindrance. His eyes were always drawn to her.

He was distracted by the songs she sang to cheer her father up. The songs she sang rang in his vague memory, shaking the ice within him. He flinched and crackled as the girl played with her hound. Her laughter made his heart thump. Her cry after her stepmother insulted her again and again, was worst of all.

The longing to hold her in his arms, to comfort her as a father would, as her father should, squeezed his chest tightly. He preferred the pain of remembering. At least he could avoid that. He could not make himself avoid the girl.

Near the end of his tenth Winter cycle with the girl's distractions, Spring came and stood with him. He let his frost angrily bite the field around him. The girl knitted stockings outside for her father, stepmother, and stepsister. Not for herself, for the stepmother said it would be a waste of yarn and the girl had to be outside lest she disturbed the stepsister. Leading her to disturb him with her cheery songs and weary smile.

"She looks like her mother."

He huffed at Spring's words, but stayed silent. The girl was the spitting image of her mother, with long dark hair and a gentle face but with her father's green eyes. She was also as kind as her mother, smiling whenever she could. But like her father, she kept silent.

"He has not changed," he snapped.

He did not like the father's silence as the girl was insulted and cruelly mistreated by the stepmother. His dislike for the father's silence and weak-willed obedience melted the ice in his chest violently. He could almost call it fury if he was willing to admit that he could feel. Frost was cold and uncaring, he had to be the same. Unless, he wanted to remember and live in pain.

"Then it is good she has you watching over her, Morozko."

He blinked. He expected Spring to encourage the father's change or berate him for his lack of faith. Instead, she said he cared, because he did. The realization made him clench his staff tighter. Quickly, he turned and walked away. He had let himself become distracted by Spring and the girl. It could not happen again.

"She will be of marrying age soon. It would be nice if she had a dowry worthy of her smile."

Spring's words froze him in his tracks and he glanced back. The girl giggled and Spring gave a small shaky smile as a tear rolled down her cheek. His heart did not thump. It ached and felt incomplete as he remembered a woman with Spring's beauty, brushing and smiling at a girl with golden hair and wintergreen eyes. A glance at his staff reminded him that he had wintergreen eyes. In a blink, he vanished.

He did not come back to Belarus and the girl, nor did he see Spring. Pride would say he was trying to be efficient. That he could not afford to be distracted. Honesty told him that he was avoiding both Spring and the girl. Even though he became efficient and deadly in his work once more, he knew he needed them. The coldness inside of him was taking over again.

It was almost a welcoming relief to not ache or feel his heart thump inside of him. To not have the pain follow him at every step, but he could not ignore the signs of his own downfall. The way his skin bit at him and the looming emptiness in his heart felt darker than the moonless night. The frost that poured out of him was jagged and sharp, cutting the area around him. At times, it even cut him, but he was too numb to care. He just walked on, and on, and on.

Soon, each step he took froze the life around him. His steps crackled and snapped as he shattered the icicles that built on him. He ignored the ice that encased his legs, stalling his steps longer and longer. Even when the ice climbed higher and higher, he did not care. He continued to walk.

It was in this icy, numb state that he found the girl once more. She sat under a fir tree in nothing but rags to cover her. The grip on his staff tightened, cracking the ice around his hands. The girl looked up, her cheeks a rosy pink and stained with tears. In a snap, he was in front of her.

"Do you know who I am?"

"No, no I do not, kind sir."

He saw the girl shiver and wipe her nose. Though he did not feel that time had passed, her face betrayed that notion. Her bright eyes were weary, her face sharper than before, her hair longer. She was older. A thump in his heart echoed the pain of her absence in his life. Revealing the hurt that his absence had allowed.

"I am Morozko, King of the Frost."

He howled into the wind, reminding himself of who he was, what he was, and what he had to do. He had no time to take care of or watch little girls grow. Even this one that immediately bowed to him.

"Forgive me, oh great and terrible King. Are you here to take me?"

Words from long ago came to his mind. Death did not watch and wait; it took without care. He looked at the girl with green eyes. He did not care for them. He gripped his staff tighter, his fingers crackling. The wind rose around them.

"Are you warm, girl?"

"Quite warm, King Frost."

She shivered and smiled as her mother did. As Spring did. As she did. He stepped forward, breaking and cracking the ice running from his feet. He towered over the girl, who wilted under him as every flower did.

"Girl, are you warm? Are you warm, dear one?"

"Quite warm, King Frost."

Her lips were as violet as her mother's before she whispered to him. Her eyes shifted from green to a familiar wintergreen. His heart raced as the girl's hair seemed to shift into a golden color right before his eyes. He gritted his teeth, clenched his staff till it cracked, letting the ice climb to his neck, anything to stop the crushing ache his memories gave.

"Girl, are you still warm? Are you warm, Snowflake?"

"Still warm, my King."

The girl reached out toward him. Like her mother, like Spring, like Snowflake.

The wind froze and the woods became barren of noise, allowing silence to have its peace in the forest. Silence came to allow memories to mourn. The girl stilled as he gaped at her, tears running down his cheeks.

"Is, is, everything alright, sir?"

She stared at him in fear and shock, but he could not focus on her. Memories flooded him and he remembered. He remembered his Marie and his Snowflake. He remembered that he was once human. Slowly, he looked at the girl, his movements free from their cracking. He took off his fur coat and wrapped her in it.

"Come, darling one."

With his staff, he summoned a sleigh drawn by six great white horses. In the sleigh lay a chest and a golden robe lined with silver.

"What is this, great King Frost?"

He led her to the sleigh and opened the chest. It overflowed with shining gold and glistening jewels. The girl gasped, her shivering replaced with shock. Something bubbled within him at her gasp, a light airy feeling. He handed her the robe.

"Your dowry, dear one."

The girl gaped as she slid the robe on. It fit and danced around her perfectly. He smiled as a flicker of blonde hair and wintergreen eyes appeared in his vision as the girl danced.

"Thank you, dear King! It is more than I can dream."

"Then please accompany an old man as he tells you his dream."

He held out his hand. With a smile, she took it, and her hand was not bitten by frost. In the sleigh, as he drove the girl home, he told her the dream and story of a man named Ivan.

Ivan was a peasant who lived in a cottage in the forest of Belarus with his beautiful wife Marie. She had golden hair and bluebell eyes. Ivan had hair the color of night frosted with snow, and wintergreen eyes. They loved each other very much. So much so, that they did not notice how their youth passed into old age. It was not until they heard the laughter of children, that they noticed the ache in their lives. How incomplete they felt. They wanted a child.

It was a dream that never ended. They had endless conversations about names and how she would look. They even built her in the snow as the other families built men. It was fun and dreaming was as fulfilling as it could be. It did not diminish their love for each other as they ripened in their old age, Ivan's hair becoming as white as snow, and lines appearing on Marie's fair face.

Then, a miracle happened. They were blessed with a child. A fragile little girl with golden hair and wintergreen eyes. A treasure that Ivan and Marie could not imagine how to cherish perfectly. When they held her in their arms for the first time, a snowflake fell from the window and kissed her forehead. They named her after that fragile, unique, perfect snowflake. Their little Snowflake, blessed by Winter.

Snowflake was as pure as she was fragile. Ivan gave Snowflake all she wished for. Any flower, story, or small toy she wanted, she received. Flowers were her favorite. Marie took care of the girl, ensuring that her skin, which bruised as easily as an apple, was fair and unblemished. That Snowflake's light hair stayed soft as it slowly thinned out. During the day, Ivan and Marie smiled and laughed with their Snowflake. At night, as she slept between them with shallow breaths, they worried how long their Snowflake would last.

Still, their worry could not surpass their joy. Snowflake loved and laughed with all that her fragile body could summon. She sang as girls danced around her. She braided flowers that Ivan brought her. She sang to her mother as she fell asleep on his chest. Snowflake loved life and the people in it.

Near the end of Winter, her friends asked to go into the forest and take Snowflake with them. Ivan and Marie were worried, terrified for their girl. Ivan blinked, unsure how to answer, and Marie clenched her hands, a nervous habit Ivan loved to see. It enabled him to put his hand in hers. Together they answered. They could not say no to Snowflake's smiling face. She went with her friends, smiling and singing with them.

When her friends came back, it was in silence. For their Snowflake was gone. No child knew or would say what happened. It was as if their Snowflake had melted and vanished without a trace. Marie waited at home, growing flowers and braiding them, hoping that Snowflake would come back. Ivan went out to find his Snowflake and take her back.

"The last words he left Marie with were, 'Death does not sit around and watch, it takes. Now I will take from it.'"

"Did, did… Ivan find Snowflake?"

The girl asked, tears in her eyes. He shook his head.

"He froze in his grief."

They arrived at the girl's home. He helped her off and gave the chest to her. She smiled at him. Just like her mother.

"Thank you, Morozko."

There was a thump in his chest, but it did not rattle or shake anything within him. It ached, but he was still standing. He watched the girl enter her home, a smile full of triumph as she showed the chest she held. Her stepmother smacked the girl.

The burning in his stomach came back, and he let it rise as the stepmother demanded the father to take the stepdaughter to fetch a dowry, bigger than the girl's. The girl said no.

He blinked. The girl, the flower who wilted under him as he towered over it trying to freeze it, stood tall against the raging insufferable storm that was her stepmother. She told her stepmother that King Frost had blessed them once and it was more than enough. She was willing to share the dowry.

The girl received another slap.

He had seen enough. Before he left, he enchanted the girl's hound to relay what would happen to the stepmother. With a wave of his staff, he disguised himself as an old beggar. He walked into the woods and waited.

It did not take long for the father and the stepsister to arrive. He noticed how the father left the stepsister a woolen blanket. When the father was gone, he approached the stepsister.

"Are you warm, girl?"

"Are you blind old man? I am freezing! Now go away, I am waiting for King Frost."

The stepsister held her nose in the air. It was a lovely dainty nose. With a snap of his fingers, frost had bitten it red. The stepsister jumped and yelped.

"Are you warm, girl?"

"I have told you before, blind fool. My hands and feet are freezing, and now my nose."

She rubbed her nose with shaking hands. He walked towards her and towered over her. She glanced up at him.

"Are you warm, little girl?"

"Get away from me!"

The stepsister's scream froze in the wind as ice formed over her body.

When her body was encased in ice, he tapped it with his staff. A blue light shimmered around the now frozen stepsister. He carried the body to the door of the house, and left it on the doorstep with a knock at the door. The stepmother opened the door wildly. The smile on her face when she opened the door quickly disappeared at the sight that greeted her.

His heart did let out a pang of guilt as the stepmother cried out, but then she touched the iced body of the sister. Instantly, the stepmother's lips turned a violet-blue and her skin became pale. She fell over, the warmth of life leaving her in a regretful gasp. Now with the girl's threat gone, he had to fix what he had broken long ago. With a nod at the shocked girl, he turned and walked away.

Now that he was letting himself remember, he found his—their— old cottage quickly. Laying down his staff, he went to the center table, where thick odd flower crowns laid. The edges of the petals and the outside of the stem looked beautiful. Though if he moved it just a bit, he could hear them crack inside.

"I could not let them die."

At Spring's voice, his grip on the flowers tightened, breaking the crown. Quickly, he let them go. He gaped at her as he glanced between her and the fragile flowers he broke. His hammering heart hurt physically. The idea that he gained Spring's wrath caused his heart to ache. Though he realized, she did not look angry. She was as blank and empty as the ice that usually surrounded him as she gazed at the flowers.

"Yet, they would not live."

"I could not remember."

It was a quick admission, but it was all he had at the moment. How did one admit that they did not want to remember? That he could not bear the pain of it? Despite how he thought of his admission, it seemed to be enough for her. She slowly came up to him.

"Then why are you here?"

"Why are you?"

She hesitated. He looked at her and saw that her once splendid features were dull. Her golden hair graying and dark bluebell eyes avoiding him. She clenched her hands. This time, he went towards her. Slowly, he put his hands over hers. She gasped, as her hands shook.

"Why are you here?"

She gazed at the pretty dead flowers. Her mouth opening and closing as her chest heaved. As he looked into her bluebell eyes, they widened and grew hazy. Taking a chance, he gently touched her face, guiding her to look at him.

"Marie?"

"I, I, I am ruins, Ivan," she admitted with a sob as her hands slowly opened. As soon as he could, he interlaced her fingers with his and pulled her into him.

"I could not forget our Snowflake, Marie. And it hurts so, so much."

Tears ran down his face as he gasped out his confession into her warm golden hair. Another sob escaped her lips as she clutched him, burying herself in his neck. Around them, the flowers wilted and the wind wailed outside. But Ivan Ded Moroz remembered who he was and where he let his grief take him. He remembered that he was not alone.

\*\*\*

**Vivica Reeves** graduated with a bachelor's degree in Media Arts and Animation not too long ago. Her other published works include a story in the anthology, *Her Story II*, and essays on the *Enchanted Conversation* site. She cultivates her storytelling with the blog

SOMETHING GOOD, and currently works at a kindergarten in Budapest.

# MODERN MAGIC
Carter Lappin

The Fairy Godmother leaned against the wall, swiping idly at her phone as she waited for her coffee order. She'd only just gotten the newest iPhone but already the headphone port was acting up again; she thought there might have been some glitter lodged inside. One of the side effects of the job—there was *always glitter.*

She checked her emails, keeping half an ear on the barista as she called out names over the din of the crowded cafe. The Fairy Godmother had been sent mostly junk mail, advertisements for useless products and an invitation to go to a distant relative's wedding. Pass. Oh, a thirty percent off coupon at Forever 21. She'd have to save that one for later.

"Rainbow Unicorn frap with extra whipped cream and sprinkles?"

"Oh, that's me," The Fairy Godmother said, pushing her way through the crowd. She'd only ordered the drink because it was the most colorful thing on the menu, but she was very much expecting to enjoy it.

She swiped the cup from the counter, then frowned. The name on the side, written in Sharpie by an overly-cutesy hand, was *Fairey Gommoter.*

"Seriously, every time," The Fairy Godmother grumbled, glaring at the cup. She looked at her watch. "They're lucky I don't have time to do anything about it today."

She fought her way through the crowd and stepped outside. Once she was clear, she took an exploratory sip of her drink. It tasted like someone had poured three packets of Splenda into an ice machine, then stirred gently before adding a few random drops of food coloring. The Fairy Godmother shrugged and drank some more.

She'd gotten out of the store just in time; her shift was going to be starting any second. She awkwardly tucked her cup under one arm and went rummaging around in her jacket pocket. It took a minute to find what she was looking for, first unearthing a half-melted candle, then a broken Walkman, then a Twix.

After a few of these false starts, she eventually found and pulled out her magic wand. It was a small silver tube, no bigger than the straw that was sticking out of her drink now, topped with a shimmering star that looked kind of like it was made of cardboard that had been attacked with glitter glue. The Fairy Godmother had sat on it the other day and broken one of the tips off, but after a judicious application of scotch tape you could hardly even tell it was crooked.

"Alright," she said, "Here we go. Dippity, Hoppety—"

She appeared in a puff of sparkles. "Boo."

There was a short scream, then a sound like someone falling over. The Fairy Godmother brushed glitter from her eyes. "I really need to work on my entrances," she mused to herself.

She was in the bedroom of a small apartment, she noticed, sprawled awkwardly across a small desk for lack of other space to be. Across from her, a bed was pushed up against the wall, next to a tiny closet with its doors shut. The floor was taken up by a blue rug and a very startled-looking young woman.

"Who are you?" The young woman asked, wide-eyed. Her face was puffy and red from recent crying, and she was rubbing her elbow where she'd hit it when falling off the bed.

"I'm the Fairy Godmother, babe." The Fairy Godmother took a long sip of frappuccino and raised her eyebrow at the woman. An orange cat, apparently startled by her abrupt entrance, peeked out from under the bed.

The woman climbed to her feet warily. "That's not what your cup says."

The Fairy Godmother rolled her eyes. "Like you've never had the guy at Starbucks misspell your name." The cat crawled further out, and The Fairy Godmother cooed at it. "Oh, who's a good boy? Who's a good boy? You are."

The cat regarded her, then hopped up onto the desk chair and leaned forward so that he could bump up against her arm. Instantly, a cloud of glitter puffed up, and the cat sneezed. The Fairy Godmother cooed again, making kissy noises at the now-disgruntled cat.

The woman reached over and took the cat into her arms, much to The Fairy Godmother's disappointment. "It's just that you don't really look like a fairy godmother," she said, sounding somewhat apologetic.

"And what's that supposed to mean?" The Fairy Godmother asked, crossing her arms over her chest.

The woman shrugged. "I don't know. You're wearing skinny jeans. I thought fairy godmothers were supposed to be, like, old. You know, with the blue dress and everything?"

"Are you talking about *Cinderella*? The movie?" The Fairy Godmother's voice was flat and unamused.

The woman grimaced. "It sounds stupid when you say it like that," she said.

"Hmm, does it?" asked The Fairy Godmother.

"Okay, fine," the woman conceded, "But if you're a fairy godmother, why are you here?"

"You summoned me." Before the woman could disagree, The Fairy Godmother gestured to the bed. It had been neatly made earlier in the day, but the covers at the foot were rumpled. "Let me guess—

something upset you, and in a fit of despair, you flung yourself on the bed, crying. Or weeping, sobbing, whatever you prefer to call it. Sound about right?"

"Yeah," the woman admitted, scrubbing at her cheeks to erase the lingering signs of tears.

The Fairy Godmother nodded. "Thought so. Classic fairy tale rules, babe; Fairy Godmothers can only appear when it's thematically appropriate. I'll tell you, it's caused more than a few headaches on my part."

The woman nodded. "I can imagine."

"You have no idea. People don't like showing emotions these days. What's with that? Like, sure, a single tear rolling down the cheek has its uses, but there's nothing like a self-pity sob-fest to draw the attention of a Fairy Godmother. It's my jam."

"Hey—"

"So, what's up? Tell the ole' Fairy Godmother what the problem is, and I'll see if I can help." The Fairy Godmother drained the last of her drink then tossed the cup carelessly aside. It bounced off the desk and landed in a small wastebasket that was full of crumpled-up sheets of drawing paper.

The woman sat on the edge of her bed with a sigh. Belatedly, she set the cat down as well. He trotted off to take a nap on the pillow. "It's my high school reunion today," she admitted, dropping her head into her hands.

"Oof," The Fairy Godmother said sympathetically, "That's always a rough one."

"I know I shouldn't care what they think," the woman said. "But it's so embarrassing, you know? I had such a rough time in high school. Everybody said I wasn't gonna make it as a professional artist, and guess what? They were right. I've sold maybe three pieces. And they weren't even good."

"Can I see?" The Fairy Godmother asked.

The woman shrugged and stood up so that she could rifle around on the desk next to where The Fairy Godmother was sitting. The Fairy Godmother refused to move to make this easier. She eventually came up with a sketchbook, buried deep in one of the drawers. She passed it over, and The Fairy Godmother took a moment to flip through the pages.

"They're pretty," she said unconvincingly, then tossed the book aside. "So. Showing up everybody at the high school reunion. We can do that. Easy-peasey. Fairy Godmother 101."

"I thought that was making carriages out of pumpkins," the woman said.

"Don't insult me," The Fairy Godmother said. "Now. First step, clothes. Show me what you've got."

The woman looked down at herself. She was wearing pajamas; fluffy flannel pants and a too-big white t-shirt covered in splashes of paint. She also had on a pair of bunny slippers. The ears were large and fuzzy.

The Fairy Godmother tapped her wand against her lips pensively. "Hmm. Not the worst thing I've had to work with..." She thought for a moment, then reached out and bonked the woman on the head with the wand.

A cloud of glitter exploded outwards, startling the orange cat again and making him go skittering back under the bed. When it settled, the floor was covered in sparkles and the woman was wearing a new outfit.

"Oh, nice," she said, looking down at herself again, this time with a decidedly more pleased expression. The pajamas had been transformed into a black suit, expertly tailored and slim-fitting. Her tie was black, colored with multicolored splashes of paint, not unlike the shirt the woman had previously been wearing. While she was at it, The Fairy Godmother had gone ahead and done the woman's hair as well, changing the lazy-day hair bun into an elegant updo that sparkled with the addition of crystal pins.

"I'm still wearing bunny slippers, though," the woman said.

"Shh," said The Fairy Godmother. "Okay, what's next? A handsome date, I think? Gotta have something for the cheerleaders to be jealous of." She looked around, eventually catching sight of the orange cat where he was peeking out from under the bed again. "Ah, hah!" She grabbed the cat by the scruff of the neck, dragging him out and holding him up in the air.

"Mr. Snuffykins—" The woman started to say, but The Fairy Godmother cut her off by gently tapping the cat's nose with her wand.

He made a face like he was going to sneeze again, but instead the air was once again filled with a cloud of glitter that obscured him from sight. In its wake stood a rather confused-looking man with bright orange hair and a neatly-trimmed beard of the same color, dressed in a nice suit and tie. The Fairy Godmother thought he was probably very handsome, but as far as humans went she sometimes had difficulty telling.

"Meow?" The man asked confusedly, and The Fairy Godmother patted him on the arm.

"Mr. Snuffykins?" The woman asked again, staring up at the man, who was rather taller than her and rather displeased with the new state of affairs.

"Meow," Mr. Snuffykins agreed unhappily.

"Tell everybody he's the son of a famous gallery owner, and that his dad asked him to escort you in hopes that it would lead to a good business relationship in the future," The Fairy Godmother said. "It'll impress them, trust me. Just don't let anybody talk to him and you're golden."

"Meow," Mr. Snuffykins said, and tried to hide under the bed again. He didn't fit.

"Probably," The Fairy Godmother amended. "Alright, what's next?"

"Shoes?" the woman suggested.

"Again, I'm bound by the narrative beats here. Shoes go last, everyone knows that."

"Who's everyone?" the woman asked, and The Fairy Godmother just shrugged.

"Okay, let's get you a ride. I'm thinking limousine. Something big and bold." She rubbed her hands together as though she was planning to apparate one right there and then.

"I actually have a car," the woman hurried to say.

"Hmm," The Fairy Godmother said, "Okay, let's go see it, then."

Obligingly, the woman led her out of the apartment. They passed some of the building's other residents in the hallway, gaining a few strange looks. Mr. Snuffykins trailed behind them, looking awkward on two legs.

The three of them, human and not, ended up standing on the curb outside the apartment building, staring at a bright green Volkswagen. It was parked a little crookedly, and a big sticker of Kermit the frog took up a good portion of the back window.

"Babe," The Fairy Godmother said in consternation. Then, again, just to drive her point home, "Babe."

"What?" the woman asked. "It's a fun car. I like it."

"Oh, it's awesome, no doubt about that," The Fairy Godmother said, "But it doesn't exactly scream successful adult, does it?"

"Maybe not," the woman admitted. "What did you have in mind instead?"

"Well, I've gotta make it out of something improbable—i.e., pumpkin carriages, etc. Let me see…" The Fairy Godmother looked around the street thoughtfully. "Ah, hah!"

The woman caught sight of what had drawn The Fairy Godmother's attention. "No."

"Yup!" The Fairy Godmother said cheerfully, skipping over to the black trash can someone had set out on the curb for collection. "It's absolutely perfect."

"It stinks," the woman said, wrinkling her nose.

The Fairy Godmother ignored her and gave the trash can a good smack with her wand. When the glitter cleared once more a sleek black stretch limousine was parked neatly by the curb, exactly where the trash can had been a moment ago. The garbage bag that had been inside it found itself spontaneously in a nearby dumpster.

The Fairy Godmother herself was similarly changed. Her blue, red, and yellow bomber jacket had been transformed into an old-fashioned black driving coat, and a chauffeur's hat sat on her head. She'd seen it in a movie once, and she was fairly certain her costume was accurate. "After you, madame," she said grandly, opening the limo's door and waving the woman forward.

Mr. Snuffykins, still in human form, darted inside without hesitation, squeezing into the back of the limo then looking up at the woman expectantly. The woman sighed then climbed in herself. Her fluffy bunny slippers were the last to disappear from sight. The Fairy Godmother closed the door for them, then went to the driver's side.

She got in, sat, and grimaced. Then she wiggled in her seat a little so that she could grab the banana peel she'd just sat on. "Must have missed that one," she said, tossing it out the window.

"All set back there?" she called into the back of the limo, then took off without waiting for an answer.

The Fairy Godmother was not a particularly good driver, nor had she been given the location of the woman's reunion, but she managed to make it there in ten minutes flat anyways. An especially impressive feat considering the reunion was based out of a high school auditorium twenty minutes away from the woman's apartment. If she'd had to run a couple of red lights and bend spacetime a teeny bit, well, that was just one of the perks of being a Fairy Godmother, wasn't it?

They pulled up outside the reunion with a screeching halt and a puff of glitter from the limo's tailpipe. The Fairy Godmother turned in her seat to smile at the woman, who was looking a little shellshocked. It had been quite a ride, but her magically-styled hair wasn't an inch out of place, nor had her clothes been even a little rumpled.

"Alright, babe, ready to party?" The Fairy Godmother asked.

The woman gave her a shaky thumbs up.

"Now that's the kind of attitude I'm looking for," The Fairy Godmother cried cheerfully, thumping the dashboard in her enthusiasm. "Now, it's finally time to do something about those shoes. Glass slippers are of course traditional, but given the circumstances I think a few tweaks are in order."

Obligingly, the woman put her feet up on the seat so that the bunny slippers were in reach of The Fairy Godmother, who was searching for where she'd put her wand in her new clothes. She eventually found it inside her hat. The Fairy Godmother contemplated the shoes for a second, then poked one of the bunny's ears with the wand.

Rather than disappearing in a cloud of sparkles like the other things had, the shoes transformed slowly, dripping glitter onto the floor of the trash can-turned-limousine as they simply seemed to melt away. As they went, they were replaced by a pair of yellow high-top sneakers, the laces tied in a messy bow. Where the Converse star should have been on the side of the shoe was instead a bunny silhouette.

The woman poked at the sneakers with the tip of her finger, as though she was expecting them to do something exciting. "Is that it?"

"What, you don't like them?"

"You made a lot of fuss about shoes being important to the narrative," the woman pointed out. "I could buy ten pairs just like this at any given Walmart."

"But these ones have a little bunny on them," The Fairy Godmother said. Then, as though she'd won the argument, she stepped out of the limo and went around to open the door for the woman again like a real chauffeur would.

With a sigh of reservation, the woman slid out of the car, trying to ignore the impressed stares that were already beginning to be levelled her way. The man who was formerly Mr. Snuffykins followed behind, running a hand through his ginger hair.

Before the pair could go inside the auditorium, The Fairy Godmother leaned out of the driver's side window. "Hang on, there's one more thing I need to give you. Perhaps the most important of all."

"I thought the shoes were the most important," the woman said. "You said they were supposed to come last."

"Nope, this is." The Fairy Godmother pulled out a plain black handbag and offered it to the woman ceremoniously. "Treat it well," she said, voice very grave.

"It's a purse," the woman pointed out, somewhat needlessly.

"Yep," The Fairy Godmother agreed. "It has your wallet inside. And a little tin of breath mints in case of emergency."

"Emergency?"

"Yeah. What if they serve garlic canapes in there? Boy would you be embarrassed if you were caught without breath mints after eating one of *those*."

The woman took the handbag. It was rather plain, but at least it matched her new outfit.

"Have fun!" The Fairy Godmother called out, then rolled up the window and settled in to wait. She didn't bother moving the limo out of the loading area, but anyone who thought about honking at her suddenly and spontaneously found their car horns to be filled with glitter.

The Fairy Godmother kicked her feet up on the dash and pulled a pair of hamburgers out of nowhere, setting one on the seat next to her and unwrapping the other. She flipped on the radio, fiddling until the baseball game came through the speakers, then sat back and began to chew.

Once she was done with the first burger, she reached over and took the other one, and once she was done with *that* she pulled out a thing of fries and ate those as well. She polished off her food without any apparent hurry, taking the time to lick her fingers clean afterwards. She then pulled out her phone and played Fruit Ninja for the remainder of the time, glancing at the clock that was set into the dash every so often. It was an old-fashioned analog thing that would have looked more at home inside an ancient grandfather clock than it did the limousine's modern interior. Nevertheless the hands ticked away steadily.

The clock hit 11:57, and The Fairy Godmother pulled the car calmly into gear. She looked over at the doors that led into the auditorium just in time to see somebody come bursting out of them.

The woman came tearing down the street, still in her fancy clothes but holding an orange cat tightly to her chest. "Drive!" she cried to The Fairy Godmother as she flung open the car door and leaped inside.

The Fairy Godmother hadn't needed the order; she was already in motion. The limo took off down the street so quickly it left tire marks in the pavement and a cloud of sparkles in the air.

The woman stuck her head up into the front seat, looking murderous. Her hair had fallen from its fancy updo, and her slacks were beginning to take on a distinctly flannel-like texture. "You," she growled out, "didn't tell me the changes were going to wear off."

"Didn't I?" The Fairy Godmother asked. "I knew I forgot something. Sorry, babe. I don't make the rules. Twelve is the traditional time. Did you enjoy yourself?"

The woman allowed herself a smile. "Yeah, it was fun. Everyone seemed really impressed. I spent most of my time talking to this one guy, but I didn't even get his name before I had to run out..." The woman trailed off, then, quickly, she whipped her head down so she could look at her feet. Two sneakers stared up at her. "Aw," she said. "I thought I was supposed to leave a shoe behind so that he could find me again."

"What gave you that idea?" The Fairy Godmother asked, taking a turn so sharply the back of the car was forced to choose between fishtailing wildly or tipping over. It chose to fishtail—quite literally as well, as the remains of the trash can owner's fish dinner were spat out onto the street. The limousine was beginning to revert back as well, the back shrinking up toward the front and the metal frame beginning to take on a plasticy sheen.

The closer they got to the apartment building, the more the car started to shrink and wobble. The smell of garbage grew stronger. The woman looked out the window, still clutching Mr. Snuffykins. "A wheel just fell off."

"Whoops!" The Fairy Godmother cried, then swerved the car to a stop. "Everybody out!"

They piled out just in time for the limousine to give one last, shuddery groan. For a moment it seemed to stretch out, only for it to snap back into place a moment later. Then it was just a trash can, and the woman was standing on the sidewalk in front of her apartment building in her pajamas and holding her cat.

She looked over at The Fairy Godmother, who had changed back into her old clothes as well. "Now what?"

"Now?" The Fairy Godmother said. "Now, we watch TV."

So they did, going upstairs into the woman's small apartment. No worse for the wear, Mr. Snuffykins wandered off to sleep on the kitchen table, though he did give The Fairy Godmother more than a few suspicious stares along the way. The Fairy Godmother flopped down onto the couch and immediately started channel-surfing, using her wand to flip stations instead of the remote.

"Uh, so—" the woman started, but was cut off.

"Where's the purse?" The Fairy Godmother asked.

"The—"

"The purse. Remember, I said it was important." The Fairy Godmother didn't take her eyes off the screen, where she'd finally settled on a rerun of *Cheers*. Sam and Diane were arguing.

"Uh…" the woman looked around, but it was clear the purse was not in the room. "I guess I must have forgotten it."

"Aw, man," The Fairy Godmother said. "That sucks." It was not clear if she was talking about the loss of the purse or something that was happening on the TV show.

"I guess I could—" But the woman was cut off once again, this time by the ringing of her own phone in the pocket of her newly-returned pajama pants.

She looked over at The Fairy Godmother, but she was still engrossed in the television.

The woman swiped to answer the phone. "Hello?" She listened to whoever was on the other end for a bit, occasionally adding in a "really?", a "uh-huh," or a, "that sounds great." The Fairy Godmother paid no attention until the program went to a commercial break.

Then she pressed mute and looked up at the woman expectantly as she hung up the phone.

"That was the guy I was talking to at the reunion. Turns out he found my purse and wanted to make sure it got back to me. He had to look through it to find my number."

"That's nice."

"Yeah. Only, he found my sketchpad in there as well. Turns out he owns a modern art museum, and he wants to buy some of my pieces," the woman continued.

"Really?" The Fairy Godmother asked. "I guess it's a good thing you forgot your purse."

"Did you do that on purpose?" the woman asked.

"Me?" The Fairy Godmother asked. She seemed to consider the idea for a moment. "Nah. See ya around, babe."

Then she was gone, leaving behind nothing but a bucket-full of glitter and an empty Starbucks cup with a misspelled name.

\*\*\*

**Carter Lappin** is an author from California. She has a bachelor's degree in creative writing and is scheduled to appear in a number of upcoming literary publications, including anthologies with

Dreadstone Press and Air and Nothingness Press. You can find her on Twitter at @CarterLappin.

# IN THE NAME OF GOLD
Claire Noelle Thomas

She crouched on the floor at my feet, weeping softly into her slender hands as I struggled to remember how I had come to be in this room, this summer-scented prison of straw.

*Ink.* The word rippled through my thoughts like the first raindrop shattering the tranquil surface of a lake. I had come to the castle in search of ink.

This was the only place I could find a steady supply of the precious liquid. The townspeople were too superstitious to trade with my kind, and few of us still lingered in these lands. Most had slipped further into the gloom, vanishing into the space between trees and the dark hollows of the earth. Those who remained had taken refuge in the deep, tangled forests, labyrinthine marshes, and wind-swept mountains surrounding the kingdom's lush heartland. We dwelled in the shadows, hidden even from one another and half-forgotten by those who feared and reviled us.

In my loneliness, I had learned to be resourceful. Gossip was easily gleaned from my hiding places on the outskirts of town, and the castle was well stocked with every necessity. It was simple enough to slip past the drowsy guards in the darkness after a lightning strike, or in the pause, like a held breath, that comes just after midnight.

I was not a thief; I always left a few coins or other goods behind in payment.

But tonight, something had changed. My path through the cool, moonlit halls had led me past one of the tower rooms on the upper floor of the castle. Behind the bolted door, I heard a muted sound. Someone was sobbing on the other side.

I could have passed unnoticed, but there was something familiar in the timbre of that private grief. The hollow hopelessness of it had resounded in my own heart, stopping me in my tracks. Without thinking, I lifted the bolt, and the door swung soundlessly open. Inside, a girl huddled into herself on the floor among heaps of straw, weeping as if her life were ending.

I hesitated on the threshold, suspended between the path I had intended and the one before me.

In my confusion and startled sympathy, I lingered too long. The girl lifted her head, and I braced myself, half-expecting her to cringe or cry out in horror. But grief had turned her thoughts inward. She barely seemed to notice me.

I knew the rules. We never spoke to them unless they wandered into our territory.

But her eyes were luminous in the moonlight streaking through the tiny window high above, and I found myself unable to look away. Tears slid down her cheeks, dropping to the floor like glittering jewels as she rocked back and forth.

"Why are you crying?" I asked the question before I realized it had escaped.

She blinked and took a shaky breath, still not really seeing me. Nevertheless, my question must have shifted something precarious inside her, because words began to pour from her lips in an avalanche, tumbling over one another in her desperation. As she spoke, I imagined the straw that surrounded us cascading to the floor, flowing into the hall, down the stairs, and out into the night.

*Straw into gold?*

It was idle talk.

The miller had boasted of his daughter's beauty, her skillful hands. And the king took him at his word. Even when she was dragged away to the castle, her father saw it as an opportunity, a chance for her to improve their fortunes. But the king would kill her if the straw was not spun into gold by dawn.

There was no one... She had nothing... It was *impossible*.

Her father hadn't meant to lie. But he was proud... Her voice dwindled into nothingness, replaced by shuddering sobs.

*Straw into gold.*

Among her people, words were slippery things. Some lies were permitted and others were not. Phrases like "Every word turns to honey on her lips," and "That horse could outrun the wind," were commonplace, acceptable. Everyone understood the sentiment behind the falsehood. But the miller's words had been judged by a stricter standard. The king's literal mind permitted no embellishment.

*Straw into gold.*

Was it coincidence?

I wasn't particularly skilled compared to others of my kind. I couldn't shapeshift into beasts, or forge magical weapons, or grant wishes. But I could spin straw into gold.

It was an empty trick, a pointless transformation. Gold thread was impractical, too heavy and unwieldy for sewing. It had no place in the homespun, sunlit world of the town, just as I didn't.

Yet for once, my useless talent was a matter of life and death.

*I can save her.*

It would be wiser to mind my own business. If I slipped away, I could leave the door unlatched and let the girl make her own escape.

But I knew the loneliness of a life spent skulking in shadows. And that was what her future would be, for it was clear that neither the king nor the girl's father would intervene to spare her life. For them, she was a means to an end, the chaff they wished to transform into riches. Their willingness to abandon her to this impossible task betrayed their greed as surely as it sealed her fate.

She still hadn't shown any fear of me. Feeling giddy, dancing on the razor edge of a nameless hope, I moved closer. "What would you give me if I spin it for you?" I asked.

The words were meant to be light, jesting. I wasn't truly asking her to make a trade; I just didn't know how to say "I can save you," without sounding arrogant and pompous.

But, like the king, she took the words at face value, weighing them against some scale in her heart. Instead of reflecting hope and relief, her eyes turned calculating for a moment. "I can give you my necklace," she offered. Her voice was still desperate, but now that she believed she had something I desired, a spark of confidence lit her features.

My phrasing had been foolish, careless, but it was too late now to rescind the offer. The deal was binding. "Done," I agreed. A strange disappointment hunched my shoulders as I pocketed the pendant and limped across the room to the spinning wheel.

Throughout the long night, I labored, counting precious seconds against the wheel's rattling rhythm while the girl huddled nearby in the straw. She did not speak to me again. But when the first streaks of dawn tinged the sky, and the whir of the spinning wheel finally ceased, she stared in wonder at the glimmering gold that filled the room. Her eyes, which had been so pale in the moonlight, now sparkled with gilded flecks.

She barely noticed when I left.

The castle was stirring into wakefulness as I crept back the way I had come. Footsteps and raised voices chased me down the narrow halls, nipping at my heels like hunting dogs until I cursed my own foolishness. I knew better than to let sunrise catch me in the open.

At last, safe in the shadows of the green woods, I paused to catch my breath and rest. It was only then that I realized I had forgotten the ink.

***

As evening deepened into darkness, I left the safety of the forest once more. The night was quiet and still, the moon a silvery orb lighting my way. Her regard was silent, but not disapproving, and her cold companionship steadied me as I approached the looming, stone towers.

Once inside, I made my way upstairs toward the storeroom and the ink I sought. When I reached the eastern tower, I heard it again: the sound of someone weeping quietly. I hesitated, time eddying around me as cool night air raised gooseflesh on my skin. But, as before, some unseen current guided me to the door.

I found her crumpled in the straw. There was more of it tonight, piles stretching toward the rafters.

As I entered, her head jerked up and her eyes filled with hope. She lurched forward, falling to her knees at my feet as she tugged something from her hand. "Please. I will give you my ring, if only you will spin this straw into gold once more."

Her voice was tremulous, and her hands shook as she held out her offering. The slim, silver band caught the sliver of moonlight peering through the narrow window and sent it shivering down her pale arms, across her frightened face.

I sighed, feeling the empty weight of another unwanted bargain. But she looked so forlorn that I could not bring myself to say no.

This time, she sat beside me through the long, dark hours. "Aurelia," she said, offering her name as a sad smile flickered across her face.

In their tongue, it meant "golden one." Another strange irony? Or had her name prompted her father's unusual boast?

I dared to ask about her life, her home, and she answered me politely, sharing fragments of stories and memories from childhood. Although her voice was kind, she asked no questions in return. And yet, I found myself savoring her words like forbidden fruit, sun-kissed and sweet, tasting of another world. Finally, the well of my curiosity ran dry and I lapsed into silence, unable to breathe life into the flickering conversation. The wheel whirred on, filling the room with gold, but she did not speak again.

When the pink glow of morning began to seep through the window, I looked up from my work, stretching the tension from my shoulders and neck. Aurelia had fallen asleep half-buried in golden thread. Tendrils of it wound through her hair and around her fingers, clinging to her as if she were a lovely mermaid surfacing from some strange, amber sea.

I left without waking her, chased from the castle by the rising sun. I was halfway home before I remembered the ink.

*** 

The third night, I promised myself that nothing would distract me from my purpose. The sky was dark violet and stormy as I made my way through the fields. Wind whipped at me, setting the cornstalks dancing like pale ghosts.

Just after midnight, I stole into the welcome shelter of the castle, following my usual route along the deserted halls. I didn't realize I was holding my breath until I heard the now-familiar sound of heartbroken grief. The air came out of me in a rush, and I leaned heavily against the rough grain of the wood, debating whether I should harden my heart and pass by without entering.

But she didn't deserve this punishment. I couldn't leave her helpless and alone on the other side of the door.

So, I opened it. This time, the straw was piled so high that even the tiny window was obscured. Only a small space at the center of the room had been left empty: a prison within a prison for the girl and her spinning wheel.

Aurelia raised her head. But instead of reassuring her, my presence only caused her weeping to intensify. "What's wrong?" I asked, as gently as I could.

"My fate is sealed," she sobbed. "The king has set me this final task. If I finish the spinning before dawn, he will marry me. If not, he will kill me."

I silently cursed the manipulative tyrant of a king as I struggled to find words that were reassuring and true. "At least there is an end to these tests," I said at last.

But she only dissolved into more tears, her body shuddering. "You don't understand," she whispered. "I have nothing more to offer you."

My body stiffened like a bowstring drawn taut. Aurelia still believed that without the enticement of baubles and trinkets, I would not deign to help a friend subjected to the whims of an avaricious king.

Why couldn't she see that I valued *her*? Her beautiful face, her luminous eyes, her lilting, musical voice. The way her hands stroked the golden threads like the strings of a delicate instrument.

These miserly people had tarnished her, broken her. She could not see herself reflected in my eyes. And to her, I was no more than the means to an end, an easy bargain to be struck.

Something shattered in me, and I was suddenly angry. Not at her, but at this world where people schemed and cozened in pursuit of brittle gold while neglecting the treasure beneath their own roofs.

A tide of bitterness surged, drowning any softer emotions I might have shared. My next words were hasty and cruel: "Promise me your first-born child, and I will spin the straw into gold for you."

It was a vulgar, offensive offer, and I regretted it instantly. I meant to shake her, to make her consider her future beyond this night. Some things could not be borrowed, or bartered, or promised. Neither I nor the king could dictate what her life was worth. Only she had the power to do that.

Beneath my bluster, a fragile flame still guttered in my chest. Though I knew what the answer must be, some reckless part of me hoped she heard the hidden meaning in my words, the question I could never ask.

I anticipated outrage and indignation.

It never occurred to me that she might accept such a vile proposal.

She paused and thought, emotions flickering over her face. I was trapped, suspended in disbelief as she considered my despicable request. At last, she took a breath and met my eyes. "Agreed."

I fought to swallow the bile rising in my throat. She truly believed I was no better than a thief, an opportunist, a predator. And I... Well, I had proved her right, hadn't I? The deal was done.

Shame hunched my shoulders as I crossed the room to the spinning wheel. We spoke no more that night, our silence broken only by the rumble of distant thunder. Rough straw rasped through my hands until my fingers grew chapped and numb. But the pain was a welcome distraction from the void that yawned between us. My spinning was so furious that stars still glittered against a black, velvet sky when the work was done.

I didn't wake her when I left. There was nothing to say. Much as I regretted it, I was bound to our agreement. Words had meaning for my people. Our bargains were binding.

I bolted the door behind me, pausing only to collect my long-forgotten ink before retreating to the welcome solitude of the forest.

\*\*\*

In time, rumors spread that the young queen was expecting a child. I could only hope that Aurelia would find the strength her own father had lacked in the face of the king's demands. Perhaps she would refuse to surrender that gentle, new life. But I could not help her, could not protect her. My hands were tied.

Months sped by, and all too soon, the night I was dreading arrived. A year had passed, and it was time to claim my payment.

The watchful moon shed a comforting, silver glow over the fields and hedges as I made my way to the castle. I slipped through the darkened halls, following the familiar path to the tower room where we had met so many months ago. The door was unlatched, and I eased it open on silent hinges.

The prison had been transformed into a nursery.

Aurelia sat in a pool of moonlight beneath the window, her hair gleaming gold in the watery light. She was rocking a cradle and humming softly, but she paused and glanced up when I stepped into the room. "I feared you might come tonight." Her voice broke, but she didn't cry out. She gazed at me steadily, reproachfully, fear stark in her silvery eyes.

I was silent for so long that she spoke again. "There must be something else you want." Her face flushed hectic red as she readied herself for a battle of wills. "I'll pay you any sum, give you anything I own, but you cannot take her."

I studied the smooth, stone floor as shame and regret swept through me. I hated the monster I saw reflected in her eyes, but I could not break our agreement. My offer to spin that first room full of straw had brought her nothing but pain. For all my self-righteous thoughts, my actions had been as miserable and mercantile as the king's.

Why had the miller ever said his daughter could turn straw into gold? Why had I been cursed with such a skill in the first place?

But that was what we had done, wasn't it, the miller's daughter and I?

I had spun her a future of wealth and comfort out of a few rooms full of straw. She had spun hope and life out of slim chances and impossible choices.

The miller had been right. Aurelia had spun straw into gold after all.

*Aurelia. Golden one.* I had a sudden vision of her, pale hair glinting in the moonlight, half-buried in golden thread.

Among my people, names had power. They were the breath of life driving us toward our destinies, the shadow of our souls, the echo that remained after we faded into dust and shadows. Our names were secret and unspoken, too perilous to entrust to prying ears.

In a heady, dizzying rush, the answer came to me. "I cannot break our agreement," I told her. "But there is another way. If you can learn my name within three nights, I will not be able to take your child."

Tears of relief gleamed in her eyes. "Thank you," she breathed.

\*\*\*

She guessed all through the night, repeating every name she'd heard in the town and the neighboring villages to no avail. My heart sank at the fear and frustration in her eyes, but I told her not to lose hope. Promising to return the next evening, I slipped away as the first rays of sun streamed over the eastern fields.

She did not guess my name the second night either, though I sat with her through the long hours. When her imagination faltered, she talked of her daughter or asked me questions about my past and my people. I answered her faithfully, but despite her pleas, I could not tell her my name without violating our bargain.

By the end of the night, we were both painfully aware that time was running out.

I knew Aurelia had asked her servants to discover my name, but their efforts would be futile without my help. I could not break the rules, but I could bend them.

As I left the castle, I strayed from the safety of the shadows, allowing the hem of my cloak to flutter through a shaft of sunlight. The movement was enough to attract the nearest guard's attention. His sharp gaze pressed into my back like a knife as I slipped through the gate.

Though my instincts screamed in protest, I made no attempt to hide as I crossed the dew-drenched fields. By the time I reached the edge of the forest, heavy footfalls confirmed the guard was following me.

For once, my limp was an asset. I didn't have to worry about losing the guard among the trees or raising his suspicions with an unnaturally slow pace.

When my leg began to tire, I settled myself in a small clearing hidden within a grove of kingly oaks. Moving slowly and deliberately, I built a small fire and seated myself in front of the blaze. As the guard lurked among the trees, I removed a piece of parchment, my quill, and a vial of ink from my pack. Then, hands shaking, I wrote my name in large letters.

There was something ominous about seeing myself reduced to paper and ink. Each loop and line seemed to stretch toward me like bony, grasping fingers. But there was no turning back now.

When the ink was stoppered and my quill was safely stored away, I stared at the paper and began to sing. It was nonsense, born of my own giddy dread. I barely heard the words flowing off my tongue, but I made sure to boast that the queen would never guess my true name.

At last, my voice grew weary, fading into the rustle of dry leaves. I gathered my pack and left the clearing, tossing the parchment carelessly over my shoulder as if I meant to cast it into the flames.

Once out of sight, I hid behind a tree and waited. Sure enough, the guard emerged a few seconds later to rescue the scrap of paper. He squinted at it and chuckled to himself. Tucking it into his pocket, he turned back toward the castle.

I slumped against the oak's rough bark and let out a ragged sigh. My plan had worked perfectly. There was nothing left to do but wait for nightfall.

Getting to my feet, I headed deeper into the forest, willing away the fear that stuttered through my heart.

***

That final night, she was waiting by the cradle with tears in her eyes. "I've learned your name," she said, but there was no relief, no triumph in her voice. Her gaze was accusing. "Is it true, what they say?"

I waited, unsure what rumors she had heard from the townsfolk.

Her eyes glowed like twin moons in the darkened room. "Will you die?" she whispered. "If I speak your name, will you die?"

I looked away, toward the gently rocking cradle. "I am sorry. I never wanted your necklace, your ring... I meant to help, to show

144

you how blind the king was for locking you away. The choice I offered was bitter and angry, and I have regretted it every day."

"You did help me," she said firmly. "Without you..." She glanced at the cradle, and I saw something shift in her face as she thought back on the words we had exchanged, the bargains we had made. Realization dawned slowly in her eyes.

"There must be another way," she breathed at last.

"Your happiness is worth more to me than all the riches of the kingdom," I said quietly. "But however much I regret our agreement, I am bound by it. You must speak my name."

"Not yet." Tears streaked her face as she drew another chair close to the cradle. "The night is young. Sit with me for an hour or so. Now that I have your name, I realize how little else I know of my mysterious friend."

We sat together as the hours drifted past. For the first time, the conversation was effortless and alive between us. We asked and answered, sharing stories and memories. I told her my people's history. Aurelia talked of her daughter and the bright future she dreamed for her. As she spoke, I gazed at the golden-haired child asleep in the cradle, and a strange calmness crept over me.

When the sky began to blush with the colors of dawn, I got to my feet. Strands of golden light sifted across the floor, pushing back against the clinging darkness. "It's time," I said, bracing myself.

"Is this truly the only way?" Her voice was wavering, remorseful.

At my nod, she twisted her hands together and stood. "I am sorry, my friend," she whispered, and I could see in her eyes that she was.

My name on her tongue was an avalanche, an earthquake. It shivered through me, and the world went very still. I felt myself slipping away in every direction, fading like the shadows still lingering in the corners of the room. There was nothing left to hear, nothing to feel, nothing but dazzling gold as warm sunlight streamed through the window.

\*\*\*

**Claire Noelle Thomas** writes short stories and poetry. She is a winner of the 2020 Trumbull Literary Competition, and her work has been published in *Mirror Dance*. Her writing is inspired by fairy tales, folklore, and the landscape of dreams. She is currently working on a young adult fantasy trilogy.

# OF WISHES AND FAIRIES
### Maxine Churchman

Poppy darted between the nettles, laughing as the rabbits scattered. Bluey thumped his foot, and sped past her towards the clearing. She turned to give chase, knowing he would slow down enough for her to keep up, and she gratefully tagged him before collapsing on her back among the soft bracken to catch her breath. The leafy canopy above swayed to and fro across the blue sky, as if to sweep it clean.

It was the summer solstice, when the fairy folk bless the flora and fauna of the forest. Tonight they would celebrate the shortest night of the year by dancing and feasting from midnight until dawn. Poppy had never seen a fairy, but she and Fern left a cake in a special glade for them every year.

Fern's voice drifted to her on a gentle breeze, and she made her way back to the cave to help with the preparations for the evening. They had their own little ritual tonight. After leaving the cake for the fairies, they would make a wish on the first star, hoping it would be granted so a new fairy would be born.

The delicious aroma of fruit cake emanated from the cave, making Poppy's stomach rumble. Inside, Fern was scrubbing vegetables for their evening meal, and Poppy gave her a kiss on the cheek before measuring out ingredients to make bread, just as Fern had taught her.

"Tell me about the day you found me," Poppy said. She never grew tired of hearing the story, and it changed in subtle ways every time Fern told it. Sometimes she wistfully recounted how her heart overflowed with love when she first set eyes on Poppy. Other times, the story was fraught with danger as she retold of the ambush of the coach, and how Poppy was thrown clear as the horses bolted.

"You were such a scrawny little scrap," Fern began. "I couldn't believe such an awful noise could come from one so small. You sounded like a dozen cats squabbling, and the din travelled all around the forest upsetting the animals. I am sure you scared them half to death."

Poppy giggled, and Fern warmed to her task. "It was fortunate I was so far from the cave that day—looking for Prince's Pine—or you might have been eaten by a wolf." She winked. "If only to shut you up."

Poppy lowered her eyes to the dough she was kneading, and asked in a tone barely above a whisper, "Tell me about the people in the coach."

Fern, always reluctant to say anything about them, let out a long sigh as she wiped her hands on her apron. "I really don't know anything about them, Poppy. This close to the border, and heading south, they must have been on their way to the next kingdom. After the attack, the two men and a woman left on the ground were all beyond my help." As a healer, it pained her that there had been nothing she could do for them. She still saw their vacant faces in the night sometimes. "Don't torture yourself like this, sweetheart." She reached over and smoothed Poppy's hair, pulling out twigs and bits of grass.

Poppy smiled weakly. "I'm sorry Fern. I love you, and I'm glad you found me and brought me up as your own. I just wish I knew who they were—who I am."

Fern kissed her head tenderly. "Enough, dear child. Let's get this broth on, and ice the cake."

As the sun dipped below the canopy, painting the leaves overhead in a blaze of golden light, Fern and Poppy carried the cake and a candle to the Fairy Glade.

Poppy set the cake on the large flat stone at the heart of the clearing, and Fern placed the candle next to it. Holding hands, with their backs to the stone, they watched the sky darken—waiting for the first star to appear.

"There it is," Poppy said, her voice squeaking with excitement as she pointed to a tiny light twinkling in the inky sky.

They closed their eyes and silently made their wishes. When the sky was black, and hundreds of stars could be seen, Fern lit the candle. They sat in companionable silence listening to the night sounds of the forest. Bats flitted overhead, just visible against the stars, other creatures drew near the clearing, snuffling in the undergrowth, and owls hooted softly in the trees above. As midnight approached, the moon cast its silvery glow on them, and Fern extinguished the candle. They made their way back to their beds where Poppy fell asleep dreaming of fairies.

The years passed, and Poppy became a beautiful young woman who grew stronger each day, while Fern became slower and weaker— her once tall frame now stooped. She no longer roamed far from the cave, and Poppy worried about their future together. What would she do without Fern? The forest could be a lonely place.

As the trees shed their leaves, Fern became ill. At first, Poppy noticed how she slept more and how her step faltered. Sometimes she would stop an activity with a sharp intake of breath. Then the first frosts arrived, and even though Poppy kept the fire blazing, Fern was always cold and shivery. Winter deepened, and Fern's condition worsened. She spent all day in bed, sleeping fitfully, her herbal remedies no longer effective against her pain. Poppy prayed for an early spring, but the warmer weather brought no relief to Fern's symptoms. Even the strong summer sun could not penetrate the chill that had taken up residence in her bones.

On the day of the summer solstice, Poppy dutifully made the cake, but Fern was too ill to visit the glade. Her skin was gray and waxy, her eyes deeply sunken, and she pressed her lips together against the constant pain. Poppy did not want to leave her side, frightened she would die alone.

"You must go, my child. There is nothing you can do for me. My time is near and I will welcome the release from this daily pain." She patted Poppy's hand; the effort seemed to tire her. "Promise you will not stay here alone when I am gone. Go to the town by the castle. Have a proper life among people." Her eyes closed and she slept—her breath rattling in her chest.

Poppy went to the clearing with a heavy heart. There was no joy in the occasion, and when she sat back to look for the first star, the sky swam in a swirl of tears. Taking a deep breath, and swiping the back of her hand across her eyes, she saw the star—it had a pink tinge. She could wish that Fern would get better and live a little longer, but it would be for selfish reasons. She shivered despite the mild evening, and pulled her cloak tighter. The pink star twinkled and Poppy made up her mind. She wished for Fern to have an easy passing into heaven, and a happy afterlife. The star appeared to wink, and Poppy hurried back to the cave.

Fern was as still as stone. Poppy gave an involuntary gasp as her heart froze. She dropped to her knees beside the bed and took a bony hand in hers. It was warm.

Fern opened her eyes. All traces of pain had left her features. She smiled. "Remember your promise," she said with her last breath. Poppy held her hand all night, tears of sorrow and relief soaking the front of her dress. As the cave lightened with the first rays of morning, she crawled into bed exhausted. When she woke, she buried Fern in her favorite part of their garden, packed some provisions, and set out for the town.

\*\*\*

A wish made from love was granted one summer solstice, and as a consequence a fairy was born. She was named Mimosa after the tree from which she came. She was small and delicate, even for a fairy, and her wings were the palest of pinks with just a hint of yellow around the very edges. Her eyes were as brown as the earth in which her birthing tree grew. Her dark hair was as silky as the finest spider webs that adorned the tree, and she wore the wispy petals of her birthing flower as a dress.

Her beauty and cheerful nature made up for her lack of magical mastery. She worked hard at her studies in Fairy College, but she was never as proficient as the others in her class. Her spells often went awry because she forgot small details when casting them, but she never gave up. "I just need to work a little harder," she told herself. When at last she graduated, she was invited to an audience with the Fairy Queen.

"You are destined to be a Fairy Godmother, Mimosa," said the Queen softly. "It is a highly honorable position. You should go out into the world and practice helping people, so you will be ready when your godchild needs you."

"Who is my godchild, Your Majesty?"

"You will know when the time comes. Keep an eye on the stars."

Mimosa set forth immediately. She danced through meadows full of wildflowers, flew over a lake, dipping her toes into the cool still water, and walked through a wood so dense she couldn't see the sky. At last, she came upon a pond that was as round as a plate and as clear as glass. A very forlorn looking frog, with an unusual tuft on his head, sat on a large flat lily pad in the center of the water.

"Hello, Mr. Frog," she said. "Why do you appear so glum?"

He blinked his bulging eyes. "Alas, I am really a prince. A wicked witch turned me into a frog when I refused to make her my wife," he croaked.

Mimosa was excited; here was someone she could help. "I cannot undo a witch's spell, but I can temper it a little." She raised her wand, screwed up her eyes and concentrated on the task before her. With a flick of her wrist, she sent a stream of magic towards the frog, catching him right in the middle of his forehead and nearly knocking him from the lily pad. "If a princess kisses you, you will turn back into a prince," Mimosa told him. Nothing bad had happened. He may not have looked any different, but she was sure her spell had worked.

The frog opened his mouth to thank her. "Ribbit." He closed it quickly. He tried again. "Ribbit, ribbit, ribbit." He had lost the power to speak. He hopped up and down angrily on the lily pad making an awful din. How would he persuade a princess to kiss him now?

Mimosa blushed. "Oops! Well good luck," she said. "You are a handsome frog, I am sure a princess will kiss you soon." And she hurried away. She must try harder next time.

She skipped through dales full of woolly sheep, flew over a mountain, dragging her toes in the snow, and walked along a riverbank where silvery fishes squirted water at her. At last, she came upon a boy. He was hopping from foot to foot with tears streaming down his chubby cheeks.

"Hello, young man," she said. "What is the problem?"

"I need to cross the river, but the bridge has collapsed, and there is no boat to take me across. I will be late home, and my parents will worry."

What a sweet boy. Surely she could help him cross the river. She thought for a moment then snapped her fingers. "Fret not, I can help you." She lifted her wand, screwed up her eyes and focused on the task in hand. With a flourish, she sent a stream of magic towards the river, tracing a line from one bank to the other.

The surface of the water froze to create a bridge for the boy to cross. He stopped crying and thanked her. Tentatively he stepped onto the ice. Mimosa crossed her fingers. The ice held, and the boy slid each foot forward before putting his full weight on it. The ice creaked and groaned beneath him, but it seemed solid enough, and as the boy gained confidence, he picked up speed. About half way across, his foot slipped, and he fell on his back. The ice was so slippery he couldn't stop himself sliding across to the edge and into the water. He spluttered and coughed, but luckily he caught hold of a tree branch which kept him afloat as he drifted out of sight.

Mimosa put her hand to her mouth. "Oops!" Hopefully the river would take him in the right direction, and he would be able to scramble out closer to home. How could she know the boy was so clumsy? Being a Fairy Godmother was so tricky.

She ran up river, with the wind lifting her hair, flew over marshland staying clear of the slimy weed, and walked past a farm where cows, their udders bulging with milk, lowed by a shed. At last, in a field high in a valley, she came across an old woman peering into a ravine and muttering.

Mimosa looked over the old woman's shoulder to see what she was looking at. There was a sheer drop, and on a narrow ledge about half way down, stood a large sheep. It had eaten all the grass on the ledge and was now bleating mournfully.

"Oh dear, Grandmother," Mimosa said. "Perhaps I can help?"

"My son will bring ropes once he has finished milking the cows, but I am worried the silly thing will fall off the ledge before he returns."

Mimosa lifted her wand, screwed up her eyes and concentrated on what to do. With a sweep of her hand, she sent a stream of magic towards the unfortunate sheep, hitting it in the middle of its woolly back. She traced a line with her wand, from the sheep to the field, finishing a little way behind where they stood. The sheep rose slowly in the air, following the line Mimosa had drawn, but it was not at all happy to be flying. It kicked, and twisted, and bucked, and bleated with its tongue straining from its mouth like a flame, and its eyes bulging and rolling. Mimosa giggled; it looked so funny, but she stopped laughing when the sheep's feet touched the ground, and it ran towards the drop again. Her heart skipped a beat, but thinking quickly, she flicked her wand and sent a stream of magic at the sheep. Just in time, the sheep stopped mid-stride and fell on its side.

The old woman rushed to the animal and stroked its face. She scowled at Mimosa. "You have paralysed it," she said, jutting her jaw at Mimosa in a most unfriendly manner.

Mimosa felt her face grow hot and her knees turn to jelly. She smiled and spread her arms wide. "At least it isn't in imminent danger any more. The paralysis will wear off, and hopefully, the sheep will be calmer by then." As an afterthought she added, "You know, you really should have a fence along the top of the drop."

The old woman's face grew bright red, and as she got to her feet, Mimosa decided it would be a good time to disappear.

Later, she wandered along a sandy beach wondering if she would ever be able to cast a perfect spell. She sat on a rock and watched seagulls wheeling in the blue sky above her. As the sun neared the horizon, they swooped down, landing on the sea where they bobbed up and down on the waves. She laid back and looked up at the darkening sky. The first star appeared, and Mimosa was sure it winked at her. At the same time she felt a yearning, starting in her stomach and spreading to her chest. There was something she needed to find, and she was sure she knew what it was. This must be what the Fairy Queen had meant by keeping an eye on the stars. Mimosa followed the pull of her yearning, knowing it would lead her to her Godchild.

She crossed rivers and mountains, walked hills and dales, passed villages and towns, but the pull took her onwards.

At last, she came to a town at the foot of a low hill, upon which stood the most beautiful marble castle that ever existed. It had smooth round turrets, windows of glass that shone golden in the sunlight, and from every pointed spire flew a bright yellow flag. Mimosa's heart soared. How wonderful it must be to gaze upon the elegance of the castle every day—how magnificent it must be inside.

She flitted among the houses and people, feeling the pull of her

Godchild. Everyone she passed seemed to be happy and excited. They were all talking about the Prince's Birthday Party, to which everyone was invited. Mothers preened their daughters, dressing them in fabulous frocks and bestowing their best jewels on them, confident they would catch the Prince's eye, while the daughters nervously hoped the Prince would fall in love with them.

Fathers watched on, with pride, certain their daughters would be the most beautiful and most dazzling at the party. Older brothers prepared their best clothes, ready to console the pretty maidens who would fail to bewitch the Prince.

The pull took Mimosa away from the town towards a river. As she approached a bridge, she heard a girl singing a melancholy song accompanied by the tinkling babble of the river. Like the water, her voice was clear and sweet, and so sad it brought tears to Mimosa's eyes. Sitting by the river, with a huge pile of dirty laundry, was the fairest young woman Mimosa had seen all day. Her hair was long and wavy, and where it caught the late afternoon sun, it shone like real gold. At once, Mimosa recognised her as her Godchild. She crept closer until, with a gasp of surprise, the girl stopped singing. Her eyes, as green as the grass, were wide and held a look of incredulity.

"Are you a fairy?" she asked.

"Indeed I am, and no ordinary fairy. I am Mimosa—your Fairy Godmother. What is your name, my dear?"

The girl got to her feet and curtsied daintily. "I am Poppy," she replied.

"Why do you sing such a sad song?"

"Oh! It is nothing really. I am being selfish." She blushed prettily and looked down at her hands, red and sore from washing the laundry. "It is just that I have been so lonely, and I wish I could go to the ball with everyone else."

"Why aren't you going? You are delightful. I am sure the Prince would love to dance with you."

Poppy's blush deepened and she indicated all the dirty clothes surrounding her. "I will not have time to go. I have all this washing to do before I do anything else." She had washed only a fraction so far.

"Well! It's a good job I showed up then. I'll have this washing done in no time." Mimosa lifted her magic wand, screwed up her eyes, and focussed on cleaning the dirty laundry. With a flick of her wrist she sent a stream of magic towards the pile of washing, hitting it squarely in the center. She held her breath and prayed she had remembered everything.

Dresses, shirts, undergarments, and sweaters immediately rose in the air and dropped in the river. They swirled and rubbed themselves clean, then lifted and twisted, shedding water until they were dry before folding neatly into a tidy pile. None of the items floated down the river, all were accounted for. Mimosa released her breath. "Phew!"

Poppy thanked Mimosa, picked up the washing, and started walking home. Mimosa tagged along.

The streets of the town were busy as everyone made their way to the castle. Poppy waited for her master and mistress to leave the house before entering. If they saw how quickly she had finished the washing, they would find something else for her to do.

Inside, Mimosa was impatient. "Hurry now Poppy, get ready for the party."

Poppy sighed. "I cannot go. I have nothing to wear but these rags." She turned on the spot so Mimosa could see how shabby and colorless her clothing was.

Mimosa raised her wand. "That, I can easily remedy." She crossed her fingers, and concentrated on getting everything right. With a twist of her wand, she sent a stream of magic to envelope Poppy.

Immediately Poppy's appearance was transformed. Gone were the rags, and in their place was a glorious gown of gold and silver. Where the candlelight caught the silver threads in her dress, they sparkled as if made of starlight. Her hair was woven into an intricate design and piled high on her head with just a few wispy strands hanging down to frame her face. Emeralds adorned her neck and hair, matching the colour of her eyes.

Poppy grinned and spun around, looking at herself in the mirror. "Wow! Is that me?" she said.

Mimosa felt a thrill of delight. Everything was perfect, and the Prince could not fail to fall in love with such a beauty.

Poppy looked down and wriggled her bare toes. "I think my mistress has some green shoes I can borrow," she said and hurried out.

Mimosa's cheeks blazed with embarrassment. She hoped Poppy would not hold the omission against her.

Outside, the streets had emptied.

"You will need a carriage to arrive at such a splendid castle in style," Mimosa said, raising her wand again, and pointing it at a large mushroom growing in the garden. The mushroom rose in the air and as it landed on the street, it transformed into a glorious golden carriage fit for a princess. Two ladybirds became horses to pull the coach, and two ants became footmen to help Poppy in and out of her seat.

Poppy jumped up and down clapping. "Thank you, Mimosa. Everything's just wonderful."

Mimosa was flushed with success, and desperate to see how it would all turn out, so with a wave of her wand she transported herself to the castle. She concealed her wings and grew to human size before climbing the stone steps to enter through the enormous and intricately carved front doors.

Inside it was as magnificent as she imagined it would be. She wandered around marvelling at the wonderful pictures and sculptures, the colorful vases and ornaments, and the fabulous crystal chandeliers.

A light touch on her shoulder made her turn, and she came face to face with a handsome man with a strong square jaw, and emerald green eyes that sparkled with mirth as he looked at her.

"I am Prince Michael. May I have this dance, pretty maiden?"

She felt her cheeks burn. "Yes," she mumbled as he took her hand and led her to the dance floor. "My name is Mimosa."

"Like the tree?"

She nodded as he twirled her in his arms.

"Indeed, your dress looks just like a mimosa flower."

They moved around the floor, and other couples moved out of their way. Mothers made tutting noises, and daughters huddled together shaking their heads.

*\*\*\**

The Queen watched proudly as Prince Michael danced. "Your brother is so handsome," she whispered, imagining Princess Phoebe was standing next to her. She would be beautiful and clever if she was here, but she had been stolen in the night when she was just a baby.

The King and Queen had been deeply distraught. Despite a handsome reward for information leading to the safe return of their precious daughter, she was never found and as time passed, the people of the kingdom gave up hope of finding her.

The Queen had mourned the loss of her child, but never gave up hope. She still sought her in the eyes of every female stranger she met, convinced they would be reunited one day.

Suddenly, the crowds gasped and separated as Poppy entered the room. Light appeared to radiate about her as the silver strands in her dress reflected the glow from the huge chandeliers. The Prince hurried to welcome her. Taking her hand, he led her to the dance floor where they pirouetted and twirled, smiling into each other's faces. They had eyes only for each other.

The Queen tapped the King's arm to draw his attention away from the game of dice he was playing. "Who is the girl Michael is dancing with?" she asked.

He looked up and frowned. "I don't remember seeing her before, my dear, but she has the look and bearing of a Princess. Are any of our neighbours in town?"

The Queen ignored him. Her hands were shaking. She pushed her way through the dancers towards her son and the girl. The band stopped playing, and everyone stood back watching silently as Poppy and Michael turned to face the Queen.

Poppy curtsied deeply, not daring to look up. The Queen grasped her chin and lifted it. Poppy's knees buckled, but the hold on her chin stopped her from falling. She found herself looking deep into the tear-filled eyes of the Queen and thinking how much they looked like her own.

The Queen let her go. "Tell me, child. Do you have a birthmark on your shoulder?"

Without thinking, Poppy covered her left shoulder with her hand. "Yes, it's shaped like a poppy, hence my name," she said.

The Queen sobbed and pulled Poppy into a crushing embrace, tears coursing down her face. She turned to face her subjects and jubilantly called. "Phoebe, my daughter, has returned to us at last."

The guests looked at each other with open mouths. Someone cheered. They all joined in, and the band played a rousing tune. Everyone crowded round Princess Phoebe, shaking her hand, hugging her. Guards finally cut a path through, and the royal family led her away to their private chambers.

Mimosa was tempted to follow, but was certain she wouldn't be needed. Exhausted from her travels, but happy with the turn of events, she headed back to Fairy Land.

\*\*\*

At the next summer solstice, the woodland surrounding Fairy Court was buzzing with the sound of wings and chatter as fairies hurried to make ready for the night's activities. For weeks they had been collecting starlight in jars, and bottling dew drops with honey. Youngsters were stringing petals on fine spider's thread, while Mimosa helped to squeeze berry juice. Other fairies were gathering nectar or searching for dragonflies. Everyone had a job to do.

Shadows gathered and the heat of the day dissipated as the sun sank slowly west. Hunters riding dragonflies returned, and expertly landed near the stacks of delicious drinks and snacks to be taken to the glade. At midnight, the King and Queen of the fairies rode out of court on jewel beetles, ready to lead the procession so the festivities could begin.

Had anyone been in the woods that evening, and looked up at the right time, they would have seen two resplendent jewel beetles leading a squadron of dragonflies, followed by hundreds of tiny lights as each fairy carried a jar of starlight.

At the glade, everyone gathered around the central stone, staring in wonder at the most impressive cake they had ever seen. It was fashioned as a huge castle with turrets and flags. Mimosa immediately recognised it as the castle on the hill where Princess Phoebe lived.

The Fairy King read a letter that was protruding from the gap between the two intricately iced front doors.

"Well done, Mimosa," he said, looking for her in the sea of surrounding faces. The crowd parted, all eyes on her, and she felt hot and uncomfortable.

She curtsied deeply. "Your Majesty?"

"It's from the King and Queen of Faraway Kingdom, sent in thanks for finding their daughter." Everyone cheered, and Mimosa beamed. She felt giddy and only vaguely aware of the jar lights and strings of petals being hung in the trees, or the food and drink being laid out on giant toadstools. She joined in the singing and dancing, and had her fair share of food and cake, and as dawn approached, she found a quiet patch of moss to settle on to rest.

The Fairy King appeared beside her and sat down, taking her hand and patting it with his other palm. "You did excellent work, my dear, and we are very proud of you," he said.

Mimosa was flattered, but worried. "Please, Your Majesty," she began. She wasn't sure how to say it so she just rushed all the words out quickly before she could change her mind. "I didn't know she was a princess. It was just a lucky fluke. I made so many mistakes, the frog, the boy, the shoes—oh! and the…"

"Hush now, Mimosa." He squeezed her hand. "I know all about your problems with details. Magic is tricky stuff." His voice was soft and reassuring. "I'll admit I'm not so good at controlling it myself." He chuckled. "But what you have, my dear…" He patted her hand again. "…is a kind heart and perseverance; two excellent qualities. Keep up the good work and don't worry so much about the little things. Magic sometimes has its own agenda, and when it's woven with a good heart, it usually works out for the best."

Mimosa pondered the Fairy King's words for a few days before deciding to revisit some of the people she had helped.

She was happy to see the sheep had recovered from its paralysis, and the farmer had put up a fence to keep it away from the drop, but she was amazed to learn how the farmer's young son had lost control of his bike in the field and crashed into the fence only hours after it was completed. Without the fence, the child may have fallen to his death.

Downstream from her ice bridge, she discovered a brand new bridge, right near the village. The boy had been swept along at a much faster pace than he could have walked, so he was not late home, but as he traipsed river water through the streets of the village, people noticed him and asked what had happened. When they heard about the broken bridge upstream, they got together and built the new one closer to the village. Once it was there, they all agreed they didn't know how they had coped without it. The whole village had benefited from the boy's plunge in the river caused by Mimosa's magic.

Mimosa began to understand what the Fairy King had been intimating: how her mistakes were really blessings in disguise. She felt the sudden pull of her Godchild and hurried to her side.

Princess Phoebe was pacing her room and wringing her hands. "Oh what am I to do, Mimosa?" she implored. "Please help me choose a husband. Prince Peter is so handsome, but he is as much fun as a lukewarm bath on a cold day. Prince Philip is wonderfully strong and witty, but his kingdom is so far north, it is constantly frozen and too far for frequent visits to see my parents. And Prince Paul is great fun, but I think I will tire of his childish ways. Help me please, Mimosa. Tell me what to do."

"I can only advise you, Phoebe, and it seems you have already discovered the faults in each suitor. Let's go for a walk in the woods to clear your mind. It might help you decide more easily."

She raised her wand and transported them to a wood where the canopy was so dense Princess Phoebe needed her full concentration to follow the path. She soon put marriage to the back of her mind and allowed nature to soothe her nerves. She breathed in the earthy scent of decaying leaves and the sweeter notes of pine. The birds sang heartily in the trees, boasting about their pretty plumage and wonderful nest-building skills, lifting her spirits with their silly words and antics.

They came to a clearing with a pond as round as a plate and as clear as glass at its center, and sitting on a lily pad in the middle of the water was a large and very sad looking frog. Princess Phoebe's heart went out to the poor creature. "Why are you so unhappy, Mr. Frog?" she asked.

"Ribbit, ribbit," he replied solemnly.

"Oh! But I do understand you. I understand all the creatures in our kingdom. Please tell me what troubles you."

With a plop, the frog disappeared beneath the water and reappeared at her feet. She scooped him up and held him at eye level while he blinked and croaked, tripping over his words.

"Well I can help you, Prince Robert. I'm Princess Phoebe and I would be honored to kiss such a handsome frog."

She closed her eyes and kissed him. No sooner had her lips touched his smooth cool skin than he became a tall man with curly black hair and piercing grey eyes.

"Thank you," he said as he swept her into his arms. He danced her round the pond while singing a jaunty—and rather rude—song in a lovely baritone voice until they tripped and fell into a heap of limbs and laughter.

"Oh it is so good to be human again," he said as they untangled themselves.

They sat by the pond and swapped stories of childhood and magic. Their growing love for each other attracted the creatures of the wood, and they were soon surrounded by the steady hum of bees and a kaleidoscope of colorful butterfly wings. Rabbits, hedgehogs, and dormice crept close, and birds gathered on the branches at the edge of the clearing. Even Mimosa could feel the love radiating from the couple, and she acknowledged this was yet another success from her mistake. Only Princess Phoebe had been able to truly understand the frog. If another princess had kissed him first, Phoebe might not have met him.

The light started to fade, and Mimosa transported them back to the castle. The King and Queen were delighted to agree to the marriage between Phoebe and Robert, especially as the Prince was from a neighbouring kingdom rich in textiles and wheat.

***

Mimosa visited Princess Phoebe many times over the years. She was the ring bearer at her wedding and she was present at the birth of her two daughters. She blessed Princess Fern with beauty and a love of nature, and Princess Mimosa with wisdom and good health.

Phoebe and Robert never missed a summer solstice at the Fairy Glade, and when their children were old enough, it became an annual family event.

One day, Mimosa asked Phoebe what happened to the green shoes she borrowed from her mistress. "What an omission! There you were, wiggling your bare toes, and I felt so ashamed, but you were sweet not to mind."

Phoebe grinned. "It worked out well, as it happens. When I returned the shoes to my former mistress, she was terribly embarrassed and remorseful for the way she treated me when she thought I was just a serving girl. She realised you can't tell a person's worth by their appearance, and vowed to treat everyone with respect. Her husband was equally contrite. He set up a school for underprivileged children, and champions the rights of working people throughout our kingdom."

To this day, Mimosa uses her magic to help others too, and although very few of her spells go exactly as she plans, she no longer worries about the consequences—knowing the magic has something wonderful up its sleeve.

✳✳✳

**Maxine Churchman** lives in rural Essex in the UK. She enjoys reading and writing crime fiction, science fiction, fantasy and horror. Her short stories and poems have been published by *CafeLit*, *Enchanted Conversation*, Black Hare Press, and Clarendon House Publishing. She is currently working on her first novel.

# FLICK:
## THE FAIRY GODMOTHER
Kim Malinowski

Flick sat in the back of the Fae Place, cinched in dark fabrics, poison berry lipstick etched on thin lips, feet propped on the table, daring the others to comment on her black combat petals—intimidating while protecting her feet. She slammed the "Dragon Piss" she had been holding on the table. "Dragon Piss" was her codeword for murky water. Flick had proudly named the drink herself, because it sounded better than whispering "I'd just like a thimble of water, please." She couldn't drink Fae wines like the other fairies because she took seven types of berries, a swath of herbs, and was prescribed honeysuckle milk for anxiety. Her mood swings and panic attacks were gossiped about, but she was the Fairy Godmother's apprentice. She had been chosen by the Godmother herself. Flick just didn't like to overthink that fact, and in truth it made her more nervous than proud. Just thinking about it made her flush—such sweat—which embarrassed her even more. She felt she lacked her usual spontaneity and impishness and reasoned that this "lack" must have something to do with having responsibility now and maybe the passion berries that she had just been prescribed.

She thought she saw something or someone familiar passing by the window and hastily looked out. To her surprise, she spied the Fairy Godmother herself. The Godmother clearly did not want to be seen—almost as much as Flick didn't want to be seen by her. The Godmother looked awfully suspicious. She darted quickly between the Fae furtively, dodging hellos and slight bows. Flick figured she would find out what the Godmother was up to—maybe a new mission? Flick was a good apprentice and a snoopy one at that. Flick saw that the sky was becoming pinker. Time to go. She had chores at home to do and then of course, the moon ritual.

Flick stomped out of the Fae Place and easily made it to the Tree. She shared it with her parents, or rather they shared it with her. Between the squirrels, her parents, and the squalor of her own lifestyle, there was more than enough to clean. She smelled food, which meant dirty acorn shells and splattered limbs. She was the "cleaning fairy" more than she wanted, but life went on. When she was here, she forgot she was training to be the Fairy Godmother, and all that responsibility and grand knowledge seemed a long way away.

When the moon began to rise, she gasped. She couldn't be late! It would kill her to disappoint the Godmother. Flick hurried off to the Godmother's circle, crashing into branches and crunching into the forest. She navigated the sacred hill—now familiar after many nights of rituals. All phases of the moon were celebrated. The moon gave the Fae gentle magic—gave them wisdom and purpose. They were called by her to care for the children and teach magic. The Godmother blessed the day and night. This was her sacred duty.

She spied the Godmother whispering to someone. The person vanished before she could see their face. Flick was confused. Usually, no one else was at the sacred circle. She felt a tremor in her chest and sipped two drops of honeysuckle milk. The Fairy Godmother embraced her and she almost choked as she swallowed. "Welcome." The Godmother began the ritual before Flick could interrogate her, but Flick knew there was a change. The Godmother bounced, acted younger—Flick didn't know that was possible.

Sunrise came and there was no mention of the mysterious rendezvous. Flick had made sure to find reasons to stay around and find out. Mushrooms needed harvesting. Of course, the corners of the Godmother's cottage needed to be dusted and pretty much everything could be scrubbed in some way. After all that, there was not one peep of news. Then, as Flick was gathering lavender, he came.

A man, dressed in even more black than Flick, which honestly said something, met the Godmother in the garden. Flick heard laughter. But she knew this was Death. The Death that took away humans and fairies into ether. But why was he here? The Fairy Godmother was pouring berry wine. Both giggled and flirted. Then they stood up. The Godmother, not even glancing in Flick's direction, walked into the purpling sky. Both Death and the Fairy Godmother vanished at the horizon.

Flick waited all day and kept her vigil into the night. She cringed, taking two red berries, then a tiny yellow seed. She had never performed the moon ritual alone. She trembled, but found she knew the words and steps. At dawn, she realized that the Godmother was not coming back. Flick sucked in her breath, refusing to cry, and walked toward the Tree. She walked slower, and slower, no longer stomping. A wave of nausea overtook her. She reached for her pouch desperately and clutched her emergency stash of honeysuckle milk. She took more than she should. Panting, she collapsed onto a well-placed limb. Her parents wouldn't understand her loss. Her breathing slowed momentarily and then her eyes popped open. Who would be the next Fairy Godmother? Flick gasped. It was her. She was now The Fairy Godmother. She was supposed to feel honored and powerful. Instead, she was horrified. This time she did throw up. She returned to the Tree, shaking.

Flick decided she was a wannabe Fairy Godmother. She was terrified she would do something wrong but was determined to keep learning and do her best. Every detail nagged her. All advice and ritual played over and over in her head. Yet, somehow, she found herself moving into routine, and as she gained experience, she found a bit more confidence.

After every moon ritual she read human news. When the sun was at its highest, she counseled fairies who had seen awful things—and decided their information might be useful. There was always human war. But this one felt closer. Fae were dying while protecting their assigned children and being traumatized when they could do nothing to help. It seemed that skirmishes and battles occurred weekly. She couldn't quite manage to understand which humans were feuding and why, but she was determined to. It would take persistence and gumption, but Flick could do anything she wanted, she reasoned. She neglected the part that it was because she was the new Fairy Godmother. She wasn't ready to think about that.

Flick could not neglect her grief or terror, much as she tried. Her Fairy Godmother was gone and she could do nothing about it. Sickness overcame her sometimes for no reason. The panic was always there. The whole Fae kingdom and a good chunk of the human world depended on her. She was not proud of that. Instead, she felt helpless.

Right before the moon ritual, Flick threw a blue pebble into the wishing well. Same wish: Bring back the Real Godmother. But nothing happened. She had too much energy, not enough... side effects, so many reasons she wasn't qualified. She had paid a price for the berry and herb regimen. She was moving on though, being prescribed different berries while growing in power and knowledge. She wasn't good enough. She threw in a grey stone. *Let me be successful. Let me make her proud. Let me save my friends...* Too many wishes for one stone, she thought. And then, the air swirled and became so dense she could barely breathe. There were guns and smoke. Dust kicked up from stray bullets. There was blood. Then she saw him. Death. Their eyes locked. There was a chill breeze and emptiness. The battle swirled and was gone.

Flick knew it wasn't because of her berries or honeysuckle milk. She wasn't delusional or that manic. She really should be anxious, but she was too puzzled to be. She was burdened by the emptiness she had felt. Her world was dying. Those humans were a threat to themselves and the Fae. And Death—what role did he play? If she died in battle, what happened to fairies? Did they become buttercups? Flick took a swig of honeysuckle milk to calm her jittery hands. Oh, how was she going to explain this one? She needed to ask… Elk and loam! There was no one to ask. She was in charge. This whole mess was up to her, and it wasn't even a test. It was real. People and fairies would die if she didn't take charge. And she was just Flick. But she had seen rapier bite flesh and cut muscle, and she knew she was going to battle.

Flick sat in the mushroom ring forcing herself to see more despite her panic. Humans would have brief triumph only to be cut down later. They had forgotten magic and whimsy. They only felt want. All of it resulted in blood, mangled limbs, crying children, and fading fairies. The humans that limped away were already plotting the next fight before they were healed. So much for battle glory. She saw Death roaming. Hand placed to mewling brow. Gentle shushing. He was moving through the mud throughout the night. Guiding, comforting—telling how proud each of the human's children would be. That meant he wasn't evil. He did his job like she did hers. They were allies? But he left with the Real Godmother, close and cordially. A stray thought whizzed past—could they be in love?

Flick held her moon ritual. This time, she saw only Death's friendly eyes. She relaxed in the circle and stomped and chanted let the mushrooms and wheat grow in the battlefield. She begged. She felt hollow, terrified, but sang to the moon and pleaded with Fae magic for all to return to right. When she finished, nothing was all right. But she knew her foe. Greed. She did not have context for why the land was so important, though. And Death? And the Real Godmother? How did they fit?

Flick staggered into the Tree, desperately needing the solace of sleep. Her things were all there. Her leaves and spells. As if nothing had changed. She cleaned the acorn shells and toppled over the pinecones. Her parents would know she was out late, but how could she explain it was for the sake of all human and fairy kind and that she wasn't just out drinking honey wine? Flicked sighed and leaped into bed. If she was lucky, she could just hide.

Flick woke to bright sunshine. She was desperate for good news. She slid out of bed and kicked something cold and hard. After cursing loudly for a minute without pause, she picked up a heavy set of armor. It was the Real Godmother's. Godmother magic was the most powerful. It was pure love and self-sacrifice. The armor reeked of her Godmother's love and courage. The real Godmother had been a warrior. It made sense, but Flick couldn't figure out what the armor was doing in her room. It must be a gift for the battle to come. She silently thanked her Godmother.

Flick understood war. At least, she did now that she had smelled it in her vision. She heaped her Godmother's armor by the pond. She had no idea when her Godmother had needed it. The armor was Flick's size, but heavy. Flick would have to practice if she intended to be useful with the armor on. She strapped it to herself and her eyes nearly popped. Heavy was an understatement. She didn't recognize her reflection in the water. She was thick and strong, definitely not willowy—but in the armor she looked fierce—a warrior Fae. If only she felt that way. She picked up a large stick and began to practice. She called on magic and will, fighting off tree limbs, dodging acorns and her own uncertainty.

Flick changed back to her usual dark garb. Moon rituals waited for no Godmother. She slid branches into a new circle and placed crystals in a grid. She sang loudly and then cursed equally loudly. "Sorry, moon." She had slammed her foot into something very heavy.

Once the ritual was completed enough, she turned her attention to the medium-sized chest she had kicked. Odd. The chest emanated her Godmother's magic as well. But there was no key. Flick sighed dramatically; it was, of course, locked. But her Godmother had seen to this as well. A moonbeam illuminated an ancient looking key in the labyrinth of keys, the place where all lost keys waited. "Thank you moon and Godmother both."

Flick plucked the key from the webbing and ran back to the chest. The key, while looking old and rusty, was camouflaged. Both the trunk and key were rather new. Flick popped one of her night berries, not sure if she was procrastinating or being a good steward of her health. Then, she plunged back into the dreamworld. Death, destruction, ash, and gunpowder—terrible screams—the dream subsided. Flick was hoarse as she whispered to the trunk to give permission. The trunk unlocked with a quick click. She couldn't bring herself to look. She would be a good steward of her health then. She chewed on the berry and herb regimen (crab apple, lotus blossom, lilac leaf, thyme, thistle, powdered rose thorn), and she thought about peeling off sycamore bark, but held that in reserve. The whole of Faedom knew that Flick suffered anxiety and mood swings... Flick shook her head. At least no one had heard her screams.

Summoning her courage, she investigated the trunk. There were a few ordinary objects. There was an old map crumbling at the corners, a shard of mirror, and a sword, burnished, but sharp. Flick didn't sense danger on it, only lingering magic. This would work a lot better than a stick. And then, tucked away in the corner, was a jar of dandelion seeds. The map was just a map, even under moonlight. There were names of places, features, but nothing that marked this is where your battle will happen. It showed the region and the places well-traveled by all sides. She couldn't see how she would use it. She gently rolled it and tied it with a piece of cloth. She slid it into her sack. The key and trunk disappeared after she had grabbed the seeds. She couldn't remember any spells or potions that used dandelion seeds—well, besides wishes. That was old magic, though.

She watched the moon begin to set before remembering the Tree. Still a mess. She ran. Shaking her head, she hurriedly entered and started mopping. She supposed all Fairy Godmothers had such tribulations? She didn't know if she meant the stuck-on food or the needing to learn how to use a sword. Both presented their trials. Before she fell into bed, she sent a moth out to find her best friend Twig. There was no one else she would trust with happenings of this magnitude. She sent another moth to call on the Fae to gather, but she worried about being laughed at. She knew she wasn't taken that seriously. She heard the comments when she had been chosen. They said she was broken, not quite right, not as good as this Fae or the next…and wrong about everything. Flick didn't always disagree.

It was still early when Flick woke up, but the moth had returned. Twig would meet her. Flick started her preparations. She drilled with the sword in the armor. No one had ever called her graceful, and they still wouldn't. She cut and hacked, parried, and prayed. Flick went on for hours, knowing she would ache, but also knowing there was no time. Magic warned her to hurry and move her combat petals fast.

After practice, Flick rested in her usual corner, so Twig easily found her. Twig looked ghastly. Pale and haggard. "I'm trying to help the children!" she said in her best whisper-yell.

Flick nodded at her. It had been a while since the two had seen each other. Twig had responsibilities—her own small children and the human children she was assigned to.

"People are being slaughtered in these skirmishes. My assigned children's family is fighting off neighboring territories. Why do they raid if they want the land? The children are terrified. I'm their fairy. How can I ask them to believe in magic when I don't want to?"

Flick nodded again. "Magic might not fix this. But that doesn't mean we stop believing in it ourselves. We must remind the humans that there is magic in life." Flick tried to sound more confident than she felt.

Twig still looked ashen but nodded. "What are we going to do?"

"I have a start. Have you seen this map?" Flick unrolled it and let Twig study it. Suddenly, Twig shrieked and pointed at a hilly region on the map. "That is where my assigned children live! This is an old map. I don't think that's how it's spelled now."

"On a fairy map, where is that place located?"

Twig brightened a shade. "One second." She grabbed her leaf satchel and took out a well-loved book. She deftly turned to the map Flick wanted to see. "Here." Flick nodded at Twig. Then, Flick's stomach turned to acid. She was going to be sick. She gasped for air. That was where the battle was going to be. All the magic, the moon, and her visions fit together. "And, on that other side, right before the mountain… that's where the other humans live that want the land?"

Twig went even paler than before. "Yes," she choked.

So, Twig knew where the battle was going to be too. Right where all the children were.

Flick and Twig pondered, refusing to meet each other's gazes. They both knew they would have to fight if they wanted the children to live. Twig was fierce and athletic, and exercised more than Flick. Flick felt less fierce at the moment and a lot more ill. She reasoned she would need more courage than dexterity, and maybe an extra pod of honeysuckle milk.

Flick chose a new place to do the moon ritual. The line of scrimmage was not easy to climb to. All sides wanted this land. There were no innocents here, except the children. She found stones and placed branches, muttering about how her circles were always oblong. When the moon was placed directly overhead, she raised her staff and a large amethyst. She did not know if ears heard her, but she whispered her magic, and called on those that lay beneath the clay. May there be no battle. No guns. Find understanding and compromise. But the land told her there would be no compromise. Only spilled blood.

Flick argued with the land. There would be peace! She hit the dirt with her staff and slammed her combat petal down. The mountain laughed. Fae weren't welcome, Godmother or no. Flick ended the ritual with ceremonial tears. The salt water blessed the earth here, whether it wanted it to or not. She faded to her familiar path and gratefully went home.

Flick slept restlessly. She had told her parents just enough and had cleaned just enough to get by. She took her five morning berries and finally got the courage to really go into her Godmother's house, not just clean it. She opened the door and hastily locked it behind her. She lifted the objects that she dusted. She knew they were hers, but would she be willing to fight for them like the humans would? That skull, those antlers, those clothes? Flick sighed. Maybe for that purple shirt she would. She hummed. It could look like she was cleaning, even if she was inventorying and stocking up on what she and Twig would need.

When the sun was at its highest, Flick entered the square. She had summoned the Fae and they had come. She greeted everyone and they stared at her. Her stomach churned. Flick knew her garb was still unfamiliar to them. Her Godmother had worn pastels. Flick never did. Everyone had been buzzing so she decided to make it clear she was not out to find an apprentice. Several of the younger fairies made no pretense and left.

To those who remained, she explained the children's plight and what she needed to stop the coming war. All three groups of humans were going to fight, and none would compromise. The children would be orphaned or killed themselves. The Fae shook their heads. Some laughed. Human problems. She was the Godmother. She could waste her time. She was crazy enough to, but she would not waste theirs.

Flick grew angry and increasingly more determined. She was the damn New Fairy Godmother. She was young, yes, they had that. Yes, they could mock her sanity, but with the berries, she was sane and their points were moot. Flick told the crowd she would be absent for a time. She would continue the moon ritual elsewhere, but she would reason with the children. She stomped off, grabbing her tote; everything had already been packed. She just wished for help. She deserved help. If the children died, it was only her fault. She played back her speech in her head over and over and the Fae's laughter; she must have done something wrong. Now there would be battle because she had failed. She just hoped she didn't lose everything.

Flick traveled and met with the first set of children. They were learning to fight with knives and pistols. None of the children mentioned math. Flick listened to each child. She explained death and pain. The children understood but felt they could do nothing. Magic didn't mean anything but glitter and bubbles to them. A pretty rock would not get land.

Flick whispered to the adults. The women and men were just as afraid as the children but unwilling to back down. They had no leader, but they were not about to have her as their Godmother.

The men and women of the other side, those of the far mountain, sparred, drilled, and their children watched. Flick begged them to reconsider. She did not want the children to experience, no, learn war.

Flick drank cider with the farmers' children after a healthy dose of honeysuckle milk. They loved their home. Their parents tilled and weeded, and the children loved the dirt, and heard the forest's enchantments. Twig had been doing her job well. But their parents also only knew how to solve problems with knives and guns. Why would they stay, knowing their children might die? She couldn't see how it was worth it. But she wasn't human. She was reminded of that moment by moment, and her marrow froze at the thought of children lying in the mud and Death singing them to sleep. She couldn't save everyone. She knew that. Maybe she could finish the war. One final battle. Some magic. Belief in Fae and love? She could taste it. She gasped as her nerves twitched. She was the Fairy Godmother now—she would figure out how.

Flick slid stones into place for the moon ritual. The first and last place she and her Godmother performed together. Ritual was ritual. After, Flick found a scythe resting near the sword. She held the scythe in her left hand, it was just slightly lighter than the sword, but she felt its power. It was just as magical. Was this Death's offering? She twirled, getting better, or mercifully not worse, and now, with the scythe, she was at least balanced. She realized she held life and death in her palms—symbolically and literally. She would spare the children. Level foe. With magic, perhaps, she would save the adults as well.

As the moon set, Flick tramped down the path toward the Tree. She saw a dark-robed figure, precisely who she expected, waiting for her. Death smiled. He nodded at the scythe. "That was made for your Godmother. I made it with pride and love. She thought you should have it..." he blushed. "You have mastered both weapons quickly."

It was Flick's turn to blush. "Thank you."

Death nodded, obviously the chatty one. "Come on. There is much to do! You must see your Godmother—I call her Mist—just so you can keep up."

Flick wondered if that was "keep up" in conversation or with his long strides? Probably both. "So, I must die?"

Death looked bewildered. "What? Why would you have to... Oh."

"Yes, oh."

"Mist and I are in love. Have been in love for centuries. I became Death and she became the Fairy Godmother. It can ruin a relationship. Anyway, she wanted more than to be the Fairy Godmother. That's why she chose an apprentice. Not so she could die, but so that she could live."

"With you?"

Death blushed again. "Yes. We've been quite domestic really. But she, well, we both think you're quite remarkable."

"Remarkable? Me? I'm just Flick."

"Precisely."

Flick was always awkward with praise and sputtered another "thanks."

Death smiled at her again, not scary at all. Perhaps, the Godmother was right: he was merciful.

"Meet me by the hill in front of your Tree at dusk."

"The moon ritual…"

"The moon will be above everywhere we venture to." He wandered past a tree and faded.

Flick entered the Tree, shaking. She knocked over every pinecone, every nut and utensil, tried to eat leftovers, but decided to just leave a note and grab her tote that still rested by her bed. She added the scythe and dumped in spells she had written on leaves. She placed her medicinal berries, herbs, and honeysuckle milk into the bag as well. She wasn't sure just how long of a journey this was going to be. The last one had been just overnight; the next could be weeks. Her note was simple, promising to deep clean when she got back and that she would be doing the moon ritual on her journey. She also made sure she had a supply of poisonberry lipstick and an extra pair of combat petals. You never knew what could happen on a journey.

She decided to do a final set of rituals. She started a "thank you" ritual and then as the sun began to lower, she began to sing the sun to sleep. She wondered what the armies and children were eating. The crops were being burned and meat was scarce. She wished the children had ripe berries and honey. She finished with a final "thank you." A whisper of hope.

She looked up and thanked Death for allowing her to finish. Death led her in circles it seemed. Had he and her fairy godmother begun to fade? She finally saw the hut and her Godmother, but not as she knew her. This was Mist. Her hair was down, and she had light, graceful shoulders. Flick didn't know what to say. She felt ill. And then, she was in that same deep embrace. "Flick! Oh, Flick, you're ready. Remember, this is for the children."

"And their parents."

Mist nodded but countered, "Adults choose violence. Children learn it."

Flicked look at Mist. Really looked. "I will do what I must. I will kill. I will maim. I will save and heal." And Flick would have to overcome the terror she held in her marrow.

Death cooked while Flick and Mist (she'd always be her "Godmother" to Flick) sipped berry wine. Her Godmother did not apologize. "I've loved him for a long time. This war is not mine. I have been in battle enough."

Conversation was easy. Fairy Godmothers never really retire. And so, she and Flick plotted and wrote spells. Death took Flick aside. "I do not want to help you fade into ether." Flick agreed; she wasn't ready to be a buttercup.

"They don't believe in magic? Any of them? Only the children?"

"It's a dark world," both Death and the Godmother agreed. "One you will have to navigate. They oil their guns. Fire them. Farm."

"So, sword and scythe—I'll appeal to them both?"

Death stared at her. "If they see you."

Flick reached into her pack and found the jar of seeds. "These are dandelion seeds?"

The Godmother nodded. "You should blow wishes with them."

Flick nodded, not really understanding.

The moon had risen. She went to the nearest hill and did the moon ritual, but when she returned the hut was gone. There was a lonely dandelion in its place and she tucked it in her hair. She realized she knew these woods. She lugged her tote and started down the path towards the inn where she knew she'd find Twig.

At the Holly Inn, no one would recognize either fairy, not even Flick. Twig had sat in the back, somehow knowing Flick would come. Her pack was full. They were both prepared for war. Was peace possible? Flick and Twig traced the map, detailing where the next battle would be. Both knew that would be where Twig's assigned children lived: right where Flick's index finger smudged the paper.

At dawn, the two fairies faded to Twig's assigned land. The children were playing ball and Twig caught it. They giggled with her. Flick took it and bounced it back to a girl, then back to an older boy, who sent it sailing back to Twig. They spoke between bounces of raids and scavengers. Their parents had learned to shoot pistols. The children knew the details, but without context, Flick decided. Twig had done a good job. The children believed in magic. It was the adults that had forgotten. She mused about how to teach them to listen to the Willow's bawdy jokes and to feel the power of the brook as it wore down rock. Could they relearn to hear the Fae? Flick was dreamily watching the ball when there was a loud bang and wail, and then silence.

Twig ran with the children; by now there were more than twenty. Twig knew the surroundings and hurried them into a barn. Flick put a finger to her mouth. "Shhh." She closed the door and walked away. The rest was up to her. The farmer parents ran into the lane. They held pistols, rifles, the occasional hoe. How could a Fairy Godmother protect them?

There was another gunshot. Then, a loud, resonating bang. Again, silence. Flick took out her scythe and sword. She had practiced but was no expert, and she had no gun. But she was going to war the human way. She marched, combat petals slamming into the dirt— anxiety or no. She found her place in line with the parents, braced herself, not knowing what was to come. Then she felt the magic of the land. The spirits did not want any more buried with them. So she swung her scythe and deflected bullets. Her sword found flesh, and while she was small, her magic was big. Godmother big.

None of the humans fell. Both sides had cuts, some had Flick's stab wounds, but Death was left watching from the side. Flick didn't want any of the children orphaned, on all sides. She rummaged and pulled out the mirror shard from her tote. For a second it reflected her blood-streaked face, and then she held it so that the sun reflected into eyes, casting small spells. Some magic, some tricks. The parents fled without their children. The invaders smelled victory. They saw the tomatoes and grapes on the vines. Saw meat as they gazed at animals. They saw and heard no enchantment. They were hurt and hungry and they thought they were alone in the world. That made them dangerous.

Flick plucked a leaf with a nod of thanks to the tree and wrote on it. She let it drift through the crowd of wannabe warriors. They slid into dream, not asleep, but in this state, she hoped they would sense the magic around them. She begged the Willow, frogs, and the brook to send magic out as loud and strong as they could. Make the humans taste the sun and stars, and for a few moments, the humans halted, confused. They watched the sunset, somehow knowing that they had almost imperceptibly changed.

Twig crept out of the barn with the children. Together they gathered enough food for the night. Flick felt a tremor in the land. "They are going to come out of that trance and kill anyone that is in their way," Flick whispered to Twig, and sighed to herself. "You have to take the children far away. The other side is coming. All three sets of humans will clash and this skirmish won't even be remembered."

"You're the Fairy Godmother, but that doesn't make you…"

"All powerful," Flick finished. "I know. I have a moon ritual to attend to. Flee."

The children saw Flick create a circle of branches, stomp and sing, flail about, but it was the most powerful ritual that Flick had ever done. When she was finished, she saw the children were gone. She paused for breath and then a shot was fired. The rival group had arrived. And the first warriors had woken from their trance. The children had been ready for battle. She had to be too. She took back up her scythe and sword and marched into bright moonbeams. At first, she thought no one saw her. Shots fired on both sides. Advance. Retreat. Flick ducked as a bullet came near. They did see her. There was blood and mud and screams. Death passed by. He met Flick's gaze. She would not retreat. He bowed his head and went through the field and lane. Flick cried to the moon as her sword hit the flesh of the dishonorable and noble alike. If she was attacked, she showed no mercy. Magic was dangerous to toy with and abuse, and Flick was the same. Bullets grazed her. Some slid past with a whoosh. Magic waltzed and time slowed. Death, the moon, and Flick, battled with the humans—each loving them in their own way.

Flick wished that she had not learned war. This was not the way. But she didn't want the children to feel loss either. Only magic and honey. Flick deflected a bullet with her sword. It was meant for her. "I am your Fairy Godmother. I am of blood and loam. My wings beat to the rhythm of your hearts," she cried. The humans glanced, halting momentarily. They heard her voice fierce in their ears, soft in their hearts. And yet, they fired again. She was a threat.

Flick saw both sides, three sides? The farmer parents had come back into the fray, and they were coming towards her. Fae were not welcome, the Willow whispered. Still, if they saw her, that meant they saw magic. That was a start. Flick began to chant and called the wind to her causing it to blow and spin about. Flick opened her tote and grabbed handfuls of leaves. Different spells went into the wind, swirling around the three sets of humans. Men and women gasped as they saw magic. One leaf caused rapture, another tears, straight hair, love… She had released them all to those that needed them. Yet the humans still tried to lift knives and pistols. Flick would not tolerate that. She had had enough. Death had done his job enough.

She called on the sky and clouds, pulled rain down in torrents. The ground became a field of mud. Humans slid and fell and fought, but now they felt magic in their bones. And then, they felt each raindrop's hum, the mud in their palms, and felt the love of the setting moon.

Flick took out the jar. She knew exactly what it was for and why it was with the sword now. She took off the lid and blew the dandelion seeds into the mud, and like any good Fairy Godmother, she made a wish. The leaf spells swirled faster, gathering speed. The dandelions sprouted golden heads at the feet of the humans—all three sets. The dandelions turned to seed once more with spellcraft. And then, Flick made sure everyone made a wish. She chanted and the winds answered, blowing seeds near and far. These dandelions grew and went to seed again and again. More wishes for the world.

The humans saw Flick—saw their Fairy Godmother with scythe and sword, armor—and they sat, knowing that even in combat there was magic. They blew on dandelions. Made wishes. Flirted and laughed with each other. Their Fairy Godmother stood on watch. She swirled her magic so that each person heard the others' needs.

At sunrise, the children returned. Twig stared at her, realizing that Flick had changed. She tried to explain the change to her friend, but Flick was still twitching from the intense use of her magic. Flick bled from grazes and felt them as she took off her armor. Death had left, so he would not help her fade away—not during this battle anyway. The adults laughed with the children, and the weapons stayed in the mud. Flick and Twig watched and sensed they were no longer needed. They faded into familiar woods—waved at each other and parted. Flick and Twig both had different responsibilities in Faedom. Flick was all too aware of the differences that kept distancing her from Twig, and the rest of the Fae, for that matter. Flick wandered through the forest, sliding off the path while taking in the battles and the bloodshed and the children's laughter—too many experiences she didn't want. Flick settled on a fallen branch, overcome. Tears slid down her cheeks, but she resolved that she would go to war again, if needed. It was her sacred Fairy Godmother duty.

She went to the Tree and started the deep cleaning she had promised. The insides had been kept up in her absence, but she scrubbed the bark and acorn shells to be thorough. After several hours, she slipped to her Godmother's hut. She performed a thankful moon ritual, placed the armor, sword, and scythe inside, ready for next time there was danger—to humans or Fae. In her side bag she kept the mirror shard for luck. She took a berry, hands shaking again. She was still Flick, but not as flawed as she had judged herself. She smiled for the first time in a very long while. She was the real Fairy Godmother, and that was enough for today. She went back down the path as the moon set and skies brightened.

The dandelions reminded the humans to feel magic, make wishes, and dream. They knew their Fairy Godmother would guide them and they knew what she looked like. She was all warrior and black combat petals.

*\*\**

**Kim Malinowski** earned her bachelor's degree from West Virginia University and her master of fine arts from American University. She studied with The Writers Studio. Her collection *Home* was published by Kelsay Books and her chapbook *Death: A Love Story* was published by Flutter Press. Flick first appeared in *Calliope* in the story "Flick the Fairy."

# THE VENETIAN GLASS GIRL
Abi Marie Palmer

Have you ever heard of the Venetian glass girl? It is a tale that may seem beyond belief in today's world, but this story takes place in an era of magic. During that time, Michelangelo was extracting giants from marble in Florence and Copernicus was redrawing the heavens in Bologna. In an age of such marvels, is it so unbelievable that a kind fairy and an artisan could make a living child of glass? I invite you to read on and judge for yourself.

On the Venetian island of Murano, there lived an old glassblower named Teodor. Teodor was a talented craftsman whose work was prized by many patrons and collectors. Yet, despite his success, he was unhappy. He lived alone above his workshop and had no family in the world. He was a shy individual, with a deeply lined face and raincloud eyes. He was friendly to his assistants, kind to stray dogs and honest with his customers. Almost everybody liked him, but nobody knew him well enough to love him.

I say that almost everybody liked him because there was one exception: Teodor had a neighbor named Biasio. Biasio was also a glassblower, but not a very talented one. He had inherited his workshop from his grandfather, whose artistry had been world-renowned and made him very wealthy. As a young boy, Biasio had attended balls and dinners with his grandfather, who had proudly shown him off as his young apprentice and heir. But Biasio had no patience with the intricate craft of glasswork. Gradually, his customers grew tired of his poor performance and went to Teodor instead. The more customers he lost, the more time he spent jealously watching as Teodor was praised for his creations. What right has he, thought Biasio bitterly, to steal my grandfather's customers from me?

But we needn't worry about Biasio just yet. Unfortunately, he will cause a lot of trouble later in our story, but first we must learn about the extraordinary things that are about to happen to Teodor.

A sea fairy named Leandra lived in the warm Venetian lagoon. She mostly kept to herself, attracting little attention and little trouble—which was just as well, because there was a lot of trouble to be had for a magical creature in those times, especially the wild, outdoorsy types like Leandra. She was small for a human but very tall for a fairy. At first glance, she looked like a beautiful woman of about thirty-five, with a scattering of grey hairs among the black, and striking turquoise eyes. She generally had little interest in the people of the mainland, with their sideways glances and marketplace gossip, but she noticed Teodor often. He spent his evenings walking by the sea, watching the horizon, lost in thought. Leandra decided that she wanted to help him.

One day, she waylaid him on his stroll. "I know that you are lonely," she said. "I have a gift for you." She handed him a small velvet sack brimming with sand. Teodor instinctively took a step back, surprised by the sudden contact. He recognized this woman. He had spotted her sometimes, collecting clams and seaweed in the shallow waters. He suspected that she was one of the wild fairies that the townspeople treated with such suspicion, and although he didn't have the zealous hatred of such creatures that some others did, he didn't want to attract any trouble by being seen with one.

"Thank you, stranger," he said diplomatically, "but you really needn't worry about me. I am perfectly content. I can't possibly accept this, um…" He eyed the bag. To him, it looked like common beach sand, but he didn't want to offend the fairy by saying so.

"It's enchanted," said Leandra, smiling, "and it came all the way from Egypt. There's nothing else like it. This sand has incredible power. Add just a little of this to your glass, Teodor, and anything you create will come to life."

She thrust the bag into Teodor's arms and vanished the next moment. Teodor stood alone in the dying light, wishing he had asked the woman her name, and wondering how she had known his.

***

That evening, Teodor didn't walk straight home as he usually did. Instead, he wandered into town, pondering the afternoon's strange events. I shouldn't even be thinking of using fairy magic, he scolded himself. If the townspeople found out… But in spite of Teodor's misgivings, the fairy's gift filled him with a newfound energy and optimism. He kept patting the sack, which was hidden safely inside his coat. The canal that ran beside him sparkled emerald green, and the setting sun bathed the tight-packed buildings in a golden glow. Could it be true? Could this unassuming gift give him the family he had always wanted? Part of him refused to believe it. But then, stranger things did happen in Venice. He found himself watching his reflection in the canal and imagining that there was a son or daughter reflected beside it.

The market was quiet that evening. Many stallholders were closing for the night and others stood chattering in small groups. Teodor walked among the tables, then stopped to look at a display of wooden toys. A purple imp watched him from a high stool.

"The enchantments on the toys last forever," he said, gesturing to his wares.

"Hmm." Teodor nodded politely. His eyes fell on a painted driftwood dragonfly that hovered at the back of the table. It was small and precisely carved. Its wings flickered on delicate hinges, animated by an unseen force. Teodor imagined buying it, taking it home, giving it to a little girl—his little girl. He could picture the expression of surprise and joy on her face. He bought the toy from the imp.

Before leaving the market, he stopped at a stall where an old woman was selling an assortment of old clothes and rugs. The woman greeted him with a grin. "Are you looking for anything in particular, signore?"

"Yes," said Teodor decisively. "I'd like some clothes for my daughter."

*** 

With a smile on his face, he returned to his workshop to begin the task. The last daylight was dying outside, and Teodor lit candles with shaking hands. Although he warned himself that this could all be a fairy trick—that no sand was magical enough to bring life to glass—his mind's eye could already see the child he was about to create. He believed in her so strongly that it was as though she already stood there, making requests and suggestions as he worked: Don't use too much enchanted sand! Don't make me too delicate, or I'll shatter!

He hummed as he worked. He measured a portion of silica and then added soda and lime. He added just a pinch of the fairy's gift, carefully stowing the rest in a locked box. All through the night, he tended to the mixture as it melted and softened in the furnace, glowing like tame lava.

By morning, it was ready to be shaped. When his assistant Luca arrived to start work, Teodor sent him home with a carefree wave. "Go, spend the day with your family. Today I am making one of my own."

Luca turned away, baffled. Teodor had always been a little strange, but this was especially peculiar behavior.

Teodor worked carefully, first shaping dainty arms, then a face, which he made with round, happy features. He imagined the girl would have a happier life if he gave her a smiling expression. Soon, he had created two arms, two legs, a body and a head. Before he sealed them together, he had a thought: A heart. A child must have some kind of heart.

He could have made one from glass, but the more poetic side of him believed that a heart shouldn't be so heavy. It should be light, like, like… driftwood. He looked at the toy dragonfly that fluttered by his workbench. Yes, that would do very well. Perhaps that had always been his plan for the toy, in the back of his mind. Careful not to singe its wings on the still-hot glass, he placed the dragonfly inside the girl's chest. It fluttered there, suspended. Then he pieced the arms, legs, head and torso together.

By evening, he had finished his work. He ate his dinner as the glass girl cooled, pondering what he should call her. Agnese? No… Veronica? No. He thought back to his childhood. His favorite aunt had been named Giulia. She had married a sea merchant who had brought her wonderful gifts from all over the world. She had always been kind to the timid Teodor. Yes, he decided. I shall name her Giulia.

Teodor stayed in his workshop until the stars came out, waiting for Giulia to awaken. Despite his exhaustion, he couldn't bring himself to rest. At any moment, his daughter would see the world for the first time, and he wanted to be there to greet her.

Teodor stayed awake, watching and waiting. The glass girl—Giulia—lay perfectly still on the workbench, showing not a sign of life. But Teodor did not give up hope. The more he waited, the more he believed in the fairy's magic, and the more he believed that his daughter would come to life.

Finally, as the sun rose the next morning, the girl moved. Her eyes came alive and blinked several times, as though she was awakening from sleep. She sat stiffly and turned her head this way and that, inspecting her surroundings. She stretched and let out a magnificent yawn.

Half asleep, Teodor exclaimed, "It really worked! I have a daughter!" He helped Giulia down from the bench and wrapped her in a warm shawl. Did she feel the cold as others did? He helped her to a chair and brought her some water and porridge, which she ignored. Teodor felt a moment of worry, realizing that there was so much he didn't know about raising a girl made of glass. Would Giulia need food? Would she be able to talk? Could she walk on her own?

Teodor perched tentatively on a stool opposite Giulia. "Hello," he said, as her eyes wandered around the room. "My name is Teodor. I'm your father. And your name is Giulia."

For a moment, the girl didn't respond. She seemed overwhelmed by her surroundings and stared through Teodor with blank eyes. Teodor felt his heart sink. But then, Giulia's crystalline face broke into a grin.

"Hello, father. It's lovely to meet you."

\*\*\*

Giulia was a bright child, and eager to learn about the world. Perhaps it was the fairy's magic, or perhaps it was Giulia's own nature, but she took to her new life as a mermaid takes to water. She accompanied Teodor on his evening coastal walks, learning about the birds, plants and sea creatures they encountered. Teodor was careful to go out when there weren't many folks around. Although he knew he couldn't keep Giulia hidden from the world, he felt cautious about how the townspeople would treat her.

He was also concerned about his patrons, who would inevitably learn of Giulia's existence. The strait-laced upper echelons of Venetian society were happy to be entertained by a talented elven jester, or to hire a diligent pixie servant, but they certainly didn't welcome the wild sea fairies who made their homes by the water's edge. Vermin, they were called in hushed tones. And humans who were caught accepting spells from the wild fairies were equally despised. If the townspeople knew of Giulia's true origins, there would surely be trouble. Teodor decided to bend the truth for the sake of Giulia's safety.

"Yes, she's quite wonderful, isn't she?" he said when he introduced his daughter to Signore Zanetti, a fellow glassblower. Zanetti was always the first to hear the local gossip, and the first to spread it. "These new innovations allow us to make such enchanting ornaments. Of course, she is merely an amusing invention—a mechanical doll made so ingeniously that she doesn't need hinges. She's not really alive," he chuckled nervously. "No, a living girl of glass could only be made with fairy magic, and I certainly don't hold with that sort of thing."

"She's quite amazing," said Signore Zanetti. "You say she is one of these new mechanical creations? But she moves just like a real girl! How did you ever achieve such a feat?"

Teodor lowered his voice conspiratorially. "Trade secrets, signore, trade secrets."

Zanetti was clearly intrigued by Teodor's words. He left in a hurry, perhaps to share the news before anyone else had the chance. When he was gone, Giulia frowned a little. "Why did you tell that man that I am not alive? I am really alive, aren't I?"

Teodor sighed. He didn't enjoy lying, but he also wanted to keep Giulia safe. "Of course you are really alive, Giulia. You're as real as anybody else. But some people in the city wouldn't... approve of how you were made."

"Why?"

Teodor told her about his encounter with the fairy and the enchanted sand. He told her that a lot of people didn't like wild fairies. "I am only thinking of your safety," he said.

Giulia thought for a minute. "I understand. As long as you know I'm real, I don't mind what other people think." She was silent for a minute longer. "But I'd like to meet the lady who gave you the sand. I have her to thank for being here too, after all."

"I don't know. If people saw us visiting her..."

"Please?"

Teodor hesitated. He had been determined to keep a respectable distance from the fairy from now on. But the guilt about his lie to Zanetti still hung heavy in his chest, and Giulia's mournful expression was difficult to dismiss. He sighed. "I'll see what I can do."

\*\*\*

The word soon spread about Teodor's miraculous glass creation. The news drew the attention of the Dogaressa, who loved everything inventive, spectacular and ingenious. She summoned Teodor and Giulia to her palace.

"Most incredible," she mused as she inspected Giulia. They stood in a grand reception room. A pearlescent-skinned fairy, dressed smartly as a maid, floated patiently beside the guests. She carried a silver tray of delicate cakes and pastries.

The Dogaressa circled Giulia regally, lifting a glass arm and then a lock of glass hair, which moved as easily as a wave. Giulia smiled and dutifully turned her head this way and that. The Dogaressa was clearly delighted. "So lifelike, and so delicate. I must have something like this for the palace."

"A child, your grace?" said Teodor, secretly shocked. It hadn't occurred to him that he might be asked to make another. He felt uncomfortable with the idea, especially since the Dogaressa believed Giulia was just a moving ornament.

"No, not a child, but something that moves. Like some birds. Yes," she clapped her hands delicately. "I would like some moving glass birds to fly around my garden. And they should be of all different colors and varieties, if you please."

Teodor smiled in relief. He supposed he could manage that. There was plenty of enchanted sand left. And after he completed such an impressive project, he would have the money to retire comfortably.

He thanked the Dogaressa for her patronage and returned home to begin his work. He sat with Giulia by the sea, sketching the birds: cormorants, plovers, scoters and black-headed gulls. Giulia sketched too, a little clumsily but with enthusiasm and flair. He chose a mixture of small and large birds, exaggerating the swirl of their feathers and the elegance of their beaks. They must be more beautiful than their flesh-and-blood counterparts.

He prepared the glass mixture that night, and began work the next day. The neighbors soon heard the cacophony of birdsong rising from the workshop. Some peeked through the small windows to see amber- and rose-colored birds flitting around the ceiling. Soon, the whole neighborhood was talking excitedly about Teodor's living glass birds. "Especially made for the Dogaressa herself, you know!" They would say, impressed and somewhat surprised that quiet, unassuming Teodor had become the uncontested favorite glassblower in Murano.

Favorite of everyone, that is, except Biasio. Biasio, who had been ignored by his patrons ever since news of Teodor's amazing glass child had surfaced. Biasio, who was angry that a timid nobody like Teodor could suddenly be the talk of the city. When Biasio's friends and assistants said to him, "You must see Teodor's birds. They are absolutely spectacular," Biasio scowled and fumed. He felt angry when he passed Teodor's workshop. He felt resentful when he saw the townspeople flocking to Teodor's window. And every time he saw Teodor and Giulia taking their evening walks, he felt suspicious. That man could not have made such a creation by himself, thought Biasio. I am sure he is up to something. He decided to follow Teodor and Giulia when they next took a walk by the sea.

\*\*\*

"I have good news for you, Giulia," said Teodor with a grin the next day. "I have tracked down the fairy woman who helped me to make you."

Giulia squealed excitedly and jumped up and down. She couldn't clap her hands for fear of breaking them, but she clinked them together like two wine glasses to show how pleased she was. "Really? Really? You know how to find her?"

"Yes," said Teodor, glad to see Giulia so happy. "Some fishermen came by yesterday to look at the birds and I asked them if they ever saw such a lady alone by the coast. They said they had often spotted her fishing in the cove. Would you like to go and find her this evening?"

"Oh, very much!"

They set out after supper. It was a warm evening, and Giulia bounced ahead of Teodor, excited to meet the woman whose magic had made her. Although she had always been contented, she had a boundless curiosity and couldn't wait to learn more about her origins.

She had so many questions for the fairy: Were there other glass people, perhaps in Egypt where the enchanted sand had come from? Why had the fairy decided to help Teodor? Had she helped anyone else in the same way? These questions flooded her head as she skipped towards the cove.

Teodor followed, glad to see Giulia happy, but apprehensive nonetheless. More than once, he glanced over his shoulder to see if anyone watched them go. He hadn't liked seeing his daughter pining to meet the fairy woman, and he knew that their visit would be impossible to explain away if anyone found out. Consulting with a wild fairy was not acceptable within the town. It was almost as awful as witchcraft, in the eyes of most. He hurried to keep up with Giulia.

Biasio watched, out of sight, as Teodor and Giulia disappeared down the path. He followed at a safe distance, protected from view by the dense tamarisk trees that lined the route. He saw the father and daughter stray further and further from the town, abandoning the well-beaten walkway for a sheer rocky pass that they clambered down with difficulty. Teodor steadied Giulia with his arm; he did not want her to slip and shatter on the rocks.

They found her exactly where the fishermen said they would. Leandra was alone by the water. She sat on a pile of sun-bleached wood, her arms extended towards the waves. She seemed oblivious to her surroundings. As Teodor and Giulia approached her, she clapped her hands together so loudly that the sound echoed through the secluded cove. A single wave rose to engulf her, and Giulia and Teodor watched with wonder as the water receded, leaving behind an enormous pile of clams in Leandra's lap. She raised her arms again, and this time as she brought them down, a gust of wind rippled her hair and dress, drying them in an instant. She gathered her skirts around the clams and hopped to the ground.

Teodor approached her, still supporting Giulia as they crossed the rocks. "Hey over there," he called. "Will you wait a moment?"

Leandra turned around, startled. But her face lit up when she recognized Teodor. "Oh, it is you." She skipped over the rocks without a trace of clumsiness. "I was wondering when I would have the honor of meeting your daughter." Leandra bent down to greet Giulia. "My, you are the most incredible creature my magic has ever made. Such life in your face! I can tell that you have a good heart."

Giulia beamed at Leandra's words.

Biasio watched from behind the rocks as the three figures talked by the light of the sinking sun. It was obvious to him that the woman—with her ugly, sea-stained clothing and wild hair—was one of those filthy sea fairies that ran wild around the coast, scaring the respectable tradespeople and entrapping innocent passersby with their magic. And Teodor seemed to know her well. Disgraceful! They had probably plotted together to charm, mislead and allure everyone in Venice with their ungodly magic. And that glass girl on whom everyone doted, well, she was probably possessed by a demon. Who knew whom she could infect with her evil enchantment? Who knew what further mischief Teodor was planning with that vermin fairy? Perhaps the birds, which he had made especially for the Dogaressa, had been trained to stab their new owner with their beaks, or pluck out her eyes? Biasio grinned, a feeling of triumph swelling in his calloused heart. He had so much to tell people.

\*\*\*

Teodor and Giulia continued to visit Leandra, always careful not to be seen. Giulia loved Leandra immensely and told Teodor that she wanted to learn fairy magic herself. Teodor was reluctant to encourage behavior that could attract enemies, but then again, he had always known that Giulia couldn't have a normal life. Perhaps she was destined to be an enchantress? Who knew what the child was capable of, given her unique origins? "I'm sure you'd do very well at that," he said. "After all, you're made of magic."

Teodor threw himself into his family life. With an advanced payment from the Dogaressa for the glass birds, he was comfortable and able to spend more and more time with Giulia and Leandra. Perhaps that was why he didn't notice immediately that his old customers were starting to avoid him.

But it eventually became obvious that something was wrong. When he walked down the street, people he knew would avoid his eye, or even glare at him. He tried to ignore it. He knew that some people must find him strange: an old man with a glass child and a workshop full of glass birds. But when he had the patronage of so many powerful people, nobody would ever turn against him too strongly, would they? Surely, after all those years of loneliness, the story of Teodor and his daughter must have a happy ending?

Alas, not all fairytales are so simple. One night, as Teodor returned from Leandra's cove with Giulia, a band of local boys blocked their path. Wordlessly, they closed in until Teodor, irritated, said, "let us through, please."

The boys snickered. One said, "Is it haunted, signore?" He jabbed a finger at Giulia as he said it. "Biasio says you sacrificed a lamb to make a demon possess it. And," his expression darkened, "he said you used fairy magic."

Teodor jostled the boys aside, keeping Giulia close to him as he pushed through their ranks. "You should be ashamed of yourselves," he muttered as he hurried towards his home.

The boys strolled behind them, menacingly close. They said nothing, but occasionally advanced a few paces until they could almost kick Giulia's heels. Teodor gripped Giulia's shoulder and walked faster.

"Does it have feelings?" said another of the boys. "It seems pretty miserable to me."

"Don't be stupid," said the first boy. "It's a demon. The only feeling it has is wanting to destroy us all!" They laughed raucously at the idea.

Teodor looked back, fearful now. One of the boys had picked up a sharp stone, and before Teodor could react, he flung it at Giulia. She shrieked as glass shattered all over the path. The stone had hit her arm. Giulia looked up at Teodor. Her shining eyes were dry, but it was clear she was in pain.

"You monsters!" shouted Teodor. "Get out of here this instant!"

"Or what?"

"Or…" In this shock and confusion, Teodor couldn't find the words. The boys advanced closer.

"We think it's you who should leave," said the boy who had thrown the rock. He spoke softly, threateningly. "This is a community for honest, normal people, and we don't like the thought of someone consorting with wild fairies and summoning demons in our midst." He shoved Teodor suddenly. "Someone could get hurt."

Teodor had no words. The only thing he could do now was get Giulia home and repair her arm. He picked Giulia up and ran homewards. The boys walked behind them, but seemed in no hurry to catch up. Teodor ran until his lungs burned, but he kept going. If he could just get home…

That was when he saw them. Crowds of them, waiting by the entrance to his workshop. Teodor was tempted to turn back, to run and hide, but Giulia's face was becoming more and more contorted with pain. He had to get inside his workshop to repair her immediately. He approached the workshop, determined to ignore the mob outside his door.

The crowd would not be ignored. At its center was Biasio, holding aloft a flaming torch. He shouted to Teodor as he approached. "We're not letting you in, old man. We know about the fairy, and the magic, and the demon child. We know about all of your plans."

Teodor shouted over the hubbub of the crowd. "You don't know anything. Giulia isn't a demon; she's a sweet girl. Whatever Biasio's told you, it's not true. I don't have any plans, except to save my daughter."

"Oh, spare us your ravings. You have no daughter. You have nothing, except this... monstrosity. We know what she is."

Giulia spoke, although the pain in her arm made her voice cracked and hoarse. "You're the monstrosity. We haven't done anything to you."

Biasio laughed. It was a deep, satisfied belly laugh. "Oh, the monster doesn't like us? What are you going to do, monster? Will you tell your demon birds to pluck out our eyes? Eat our crops? Will you stab me with that dagger you have there?" He gestured to the sharp edge of Giulia's shattered arm and grinned a terrible grin. "I knew from the start that you couldn't be trusted. Others may have fallen for that charming smile, but I always knew you were only a cheap trick. A puppet possessed by an evil spirit. And now everyone else can see it too."

"That's enough!" Teodor found his voice. "You people have no authority to be here. I must get my daughter inside. She's injured."

"Oh, must you?" Biasio raised his eyebrows mockingly. "Well then, by all means, be my guest." He gestured with a mocking flourish to Teodor's front door. Teodor approached it cautiously.

Ouch! The iron handle was red-hot. Inside, Teodor could hear a faint crackling. He stared at Biasio, aghast. "What have you done?"

"I've given you what you deserve, old man. You should have stayed in your pathetic little home by yourself, where you belong. You should never have tried to rival me. You should have stayed in your place." His face twisted angrily. "But you didn't, so I'm going to put you there."

Biasio kicked open the door theatrically. A plume of smoke erupted from the entrance. Teodor stumbled away from the smoke, clutching Giulia close. There were only a few flames so far, but the fire was spreading even as they watched. Through the smoke, Teodor could see his glass birds flying in an erratic, panicked circuit around the room. They were sure to smash themselves against the walls with the smoke blocking their view. Teodor wished he could help them, but his first thought was of rescuing Giulia from this nightmarish scene. He could mend her arm another time, somewhere safe. For now, they had to run far away.

Teodor took a few clumsy steps backwards, but the crowd had swarmed on all sides and there was no way out.

Biasio grabbed Teodor and Giulia by their collars. "I'm doing this for everyone's safety," he growled. "Except yours, of course." He yanked them towards the soot-choked open door, smirking grimly.

But Giulia fought back savagely. Her glass skin was hard, and she flailed at Biasio, swatting his face and stomping on his feet. Biasio let out an enraged howl.

"Keep still, you little beast!"

Giulia screwed up her face and jabbed her arm at Biasio. It was her broken arm, and its sharp edges shredded his clothes and skin. Blood bloomed across his doublet. He shrieked.

"She stabbed me! She's trying to kill me; you all saw it!"

The crowd hung back, reluctant to respond. Biasio had promised them a monster, but all they saw was an old man and an injured little girl in danger. Biasio continued to force his victims towards the smoking doorway, oblivious to the crowd's reaction. When Teodor struggled against his grip, Biasio struck him across the face and threw his two captives to the ground. Teodor, barely conscious, heard the sound of glass splintering. Giulia's arm was almost completely destroyed now. All that was left of it was a jagged shard protruding from her shoulder. Biasio glowered down at them.

Teodor coughed and spluttered as the smoke billowed from the doorway. He was clearly struggling to breathe. Biasio smiled triumphantly at Teodor's weakness, and Giulia saw red. She raised her smashed arm and lunged at Biasio, driving the jagged fragment into his thigh. Biasio screamed.

Teodor, through a haze of disorientation, watched his daughter.

She stood up shakily, blood trickling down the blade of her arm. Her eyes were hard. Biasio crumpled to the floor, pressing on his wound and groaning. Giulia raised her arm to strike him again, but Teodor held her back weakly.

"Giulia, no. This isn't how I made you."

Giulia looked at Teodor in anguish. "I'm only defending us, father. He wants to kill us. He's evil."

"But you're not. You're a good person, Giulia. You have to act like one."

Giulia paused, surveying the grimacing Biasio, still bent over on the floor. She sank down to the floor next to Teodor. Though her eyes couldn't make tears, she sobbed uncontrollably.

A woman's voice rang out from behind the crowd. "He's right, Giulia. You're a sweet, kind girl; you shouldn't go around stabbing people—not even pathetic low-lifes like Biasio." Teodor and Giulia looked up to see who had spoken. It was Leandra. She stepped forward, parting the crowd as if by magic. "Fortunately for you, I am not so kind. As you have been told many times, I am an evil, feral wild fairy, and I have no problem taking revenge on those who hurt my friends."

And with that, she raised her arms high in the air and clapped once, so swiftly that it created a sudden breeze. For a few seconds, there was silence. Then the thundering sound of water overwhelmed them, and a great wave rose over the crowd. Some members of the mob, who had already been backing away from the scene, ran away quickly enough to escape the deluge. Biasio lay, cursing, on the ground. As the water crashed down, Teodor, Leandra and Giulia huddled together tightly, anchoring each other against the ocean's mighty pull.

***

Nobody knows what happened to the three of them after that. Some say they left Venice. There were tales of strange magic in Val Camonica several years later. Some say they retreated to the lagoons, or hid in coastal caves, and emerged only at night. Some say the wave dragged them out to sea, and all that was left of the little glass girl were some fine glass shards carried in by the morning tide. To this day, visitors to Venice report sightings of a peculiar type of dragonfly that lives in a secluded cove on the island of Murano. Its wings look like finely-carved driftwood, and as it flies among the waves, the water dances and parts as if by magic.

***

**Abi Marie Palmer** writes stories inspired by folklore, urban legends and cheesy monster movies. She lives in a cosy attic by the sea and teaches English by day. You can find more of her work at abimariepalmer.com.

## ABOUT THE ANTHOLOGIST

**Kate Wolford** is a writer, editor, and blogger living in the Midwest. Fairy tales are her specialty. Previous books include *Beyond the Glass Slipper: Ten Neglected Fairy Tales to Fall in Love With*, *Krampusnacht: Twelve Nights of Krampus*, *Frozen Fairy Tales*, and *Skull and Pestle: New Tales of Baba Yaga* all published by World Weaver Press. She was the founder of *Enchanted Conversation: A Fairy Tale Magazine*, at fairytalemagazine.com.

Thank you for reading!

We hope you'll leave an honest review at Amazon, Goodreads, or wherever you discuss books online.

Leaving a review helps readers like you discover they books they'll love, and shows support for the authors and editors who worked so hard to create this book.

Please sign up for our newsletter for news about upcoming titles, submission opportunities, special discounts, & more.

WorldWeaverPress.com/newsletter-signup

## Krampusnacht: Twelve Nights of Krampus
A Christmas Krampus anthology
Edited by Kate Wolford

For bad children, a lump of coal from Santa is positively light punishment when Krampus is ready and waiting to beat them with a stick, wrap them in chains, and drag them down to hell—all with St. Nick's encouragement and approval.

*Krampusnacht* holds within its pages twelve tales of Krampus triumphant, usurped, befriended, and much more. From evil children (and adults) who get their due, to those who pull one over on the ancient "Christmas Devil." From historic Europe, to the North Pole, to present day American suburbia, these all new stories embark on a revitalization of the Krampus tradition.

Whether you choose to read *Krampusnacht* over twelve dark and scary nights or devour it in one *nacht* of joy and terror, these stories are sure to add chills and magic to any winter's reading.

"From funny to pure terror…This is a must-read for the upcoming holiday season."
— Bitten By Books

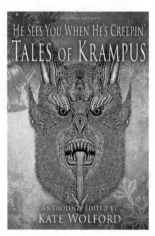

## HE SEES YOU WHEN HE'S CREEPIN': TALES OF KRAMPUS
Edited by Kate Wolford

Krampus is the cloven-hoofed, curly-horned, and long-tongued dark companion of St. Nick. Sometimes a hero, sometimes a villain, within these pages, he's always more than just a sidekick. You'll meet manifestations of Santa's dark servant as he goes toe-to-toe with a bratty Cinderella, a guitar-slinging girl hero, a coffee shop-owning hipster, and sometimes even St. Nick himself. Whether you want a dash of horror or a hint of joy and redemption, these 12 new tales of Krampus will help you gear up for the most "wonderful" time of the year.

Featuring original stories by Steven Grimm, Lissa Marie Redmond, Beth Mann, Anya J. Davis, E.J. Hagadorn, S.E. Foley, Brad P. Christy, Ross Baxter, Nancy Brewka-Clark, Tamsin Showbrook, E.M. Eastick, and Jude Tulli.

"These stories were well chosen, and this anthology is perfect for those of you that like Nightmare Before Christmas and other Halloween/Christmas crosses. This one is worth checking out if you like unique and interesting stories."
—Hollie Ohs Book Reviews

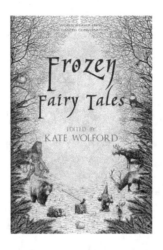

# FROZEN FAIRY TALES
Edited By Kate Wolford

**Winter is not coming. Winter is here.**

As unique and beautifully formed as a snowflake, each of these fifteen stories spins a brand new tale or offers a fresh take on an old favorite like Jack Frost, The Snow Queen, or The Frog King. From a drafty castle to a blustery Japanese village, from a snow-packed road to the cozy hearth of a farmhouse, from an empty coffee house in Buffalo, New York, to a cold night outside a university library, these stories fully explore the perils and possibilities of the snow, wind, ice, and bone-chilling cold that traditional fairy tale characters seldom encounter.

In the bleak midwinter, heed the irresistible call of fairy tales. Just open these pages, snuggle down, and wait for an icy blast of fantasy to carry you away. With all new stories of love, adventure, sorrow, and triumph by Tina Anton, Amanda Bergloff, Gavin Bradley, L.A. Christensen, Steven Grimm, Christina Ruth Johnson, Rowan Lindstrom, Alison McBain, Aimee Ogden, J. Patrick Pazdziora, Lissa Marie Redmond, Anna Salonen, Lissa Sloan, Charity Tahmaseb, and David Turnbull to help you dream through the cold days and nights of this most dreaded season.

# BEYOND THE GLASS SLIPPER

Ten Neglected Fairy Tales to Fall In Love With
With Annotations by Kate Wolford

*Some fairy tales everyone knows—these aren't those tales.* These are tales of kings who get deposed and pigs who get married. These are ten tales, much neglected. Editor of *Enchanted Conversation: A Fairy Tale Magazine*, Kate Wolford, introduces and annotates each tale in a manner that won't leave novices of fairy tale studies lost in the woods to grandmother's house, yet with a depth of research and a delight in posing intriguing puzzles that will cause folklorists and savvy readers to find this collection a delicious new delicacy.

*Beyond the Glass Slipper* is about more than just reading fairy tales—it's about connecting to them. It's about thinking of the fairy tale as a precursor to *Saturday Night Live* as much as it is to any princess-movie franchise: the tales within these pages abound with outrageous spectacle and absurdist vignettes, ripe with humor that pokes fun at ourselves and our society.

Never stuffy or pedantic, Kate Wolford proves she's the college professor you always wish you had: smart, nurturing, and plugged into pop culture.

CPSIA information can be obtained
at www.ICGtesting.com
Printed in the USA
LVHW080337020422
714939LV00013B/534